Disnarration and the Unmentioned in Fact and Fiction

Marina Lambrou

Disnarration and the Unmentioned in Fact and Fiction

To Alan
– friend and co-author. I can
finally give you my single
authored book, which I
hope you'll enjoy!
Can't wait to meet up
– Marina
(May 20)

palgrave
macmillan

Marina Lambrou
Department of Humanities
Kingston University
Surrey, UK

ISBN 978-1-137-50777-8 ISBN 978-1-137-50778-5 (eBook)
https://doi.org/10.1057/978-1-137-50778-5

Library of Congress Control Number: 2019931741

This Palgrave Pivot imprint is published by the registered company Springer Nature Limited
The registered company address is: The Campus, 4 Crinan Street, London, N1 9XW, United Kingdom

To Costas and Chrystalleni Lambrou. You gave me a love of stories, a sense of wonder, a way with words. This is for you.

Acknowledgements

I would like to thank everyone who has helped me develop this book whether you are aware of it or not. I would like to thank, especially, my fellow stylisticians for the numerous informal conversations about *what might have been but is not*, including friends and colleagues at the 2014 Poetics and Linguistics Association (PALA) conference in Maribor, who responded positively to my paper and gave me the impetus to develop my ideas into this book. I first discovered Tobias Wolff's short story *Bullet in the Brain* at the 2013 Narrative Matters conference in Paris, so thank you too.

I would like to thank the (now grown up) children of Manor Hill Greek School in North London for participating in my research and giving me their wonderful, disnarrated personal experiences, which first prompted my interest in this dimension of storytelling.

I would also like to thank Palgrave for the opportunity to publish my work with them (and for their patience throughout this undertaking). My thanks also go to Kingston University for my sabbatical which gave me the valuable time and space to write all this down.

Last but not least, I want to thank Gerald Prince for starting all of this. If it was not for his work on the unnarratable, I could not have written this book.

Contents

List of Tables

CHAPTER 1

Introduction to *Disnarration and the Unmentioned in Fact and Fiction*

Abstract *Disnarration and the Unmentioned in Fact and Fiction* explores the presence of a dimension of storytelling described as "the disnarrated" (Prince 1988) across three genres of texts: personal narratives; news stories and fiction (literary and film). The main aim is to offer a broad discussion of disnarration 'the events that do not happen but, nonetheless, are referred to' (Prince 1988) beyond literary fiction to include factual texts where this dimension of storytelling has not been fully explored to understand why disnarration is so pervasive. Other aims include identifying the discourse of disnarration to describe the creative absences and counterfactual divergences in these modes of storytelling. This chapter provides an overview of the chapters and scope of the book.

Keywords Disnarration · Literary fiction · Personal experience · News stories · Counterfactuality

> When I was younger, I could remember anything, whether it had happened or not; but my faculties are decaying now and soon I shall be so I cannot remember any but the things that never happened. Mark Twain (1924: 96)

M. Lambrou, *Disnarration and the Unmentioned in Fact and Fiction*,
https://doi.org/10.1057/978-1-137-50778-5_1

Aims and Scope of Book

Why is it that stories where events that are explicitly referred to but do not happen are nevertheless considered to be tellable? Why are stories where something could have happened, such as on near misses in news stories, or experiences about something almost happening in personal narratives, or gaps and omissions as well as counterfactual scenarios in film and literary fiction, be seen as newsworthy, tellable and narratable? *Disnarration and the Unmentioned in Fact and Fiction* sets out to discuss the continuing 'fascination of what doesn't happen' (Dannenberg 2014) by examining Prince's (1988) thought-provoking narrative dimension 'the disnarrated', which describes 'terms, phrases and passages that consider what did or does not take place' (p. 3). Discussions also draw on Warhol's (2005, 2007, 2010) work on narrative refusals in Victorian fiction which extends Prince's concept, where omissions are as communicative by their very absence as the text that is present. Dannenberg's concept of *counterfactual divergence* which generates *what if* scenarios when narrators, characters and plots follow alternative paths are also examined as are the forking paths and the multiple plot options that open as a consequence. Central to this exploration of unusual narrative techniques are the factual and fictional narratives, specifically chosen from across a range of genres: natural narratives, media new stories, a short story and a hugely successful Hollywood film to show the pervasiveness of disnarration and narrative gaps. This book sets out to understand the range of linguistic and literary techniques for communicating disnarration, textual gaps, refusals and hypothetical scenarios in an attempt to understand their importance and their relevance as part of our repertoire of storytelling.

As the title of this book suggests, *Disnarration and the Unmentioned in Fact and Fiction* attempts to examine the presence of disnarration as an unconventional storytelling strategy. Situated within the study of narratology, existing discussions of disnarration have tended to focus on literary fiction, consisting of characters inhabiting a storyworld, and enacting a series of temporally ordered and casually linked events to form a plot. This book differs in that it offers insights into disnarration as a narrative technique that goes beyond fictional texts to also consider factually based narratives such as oral narratives of personal experience and news narratives where the central concept of truth and the presence of crisis are important factors for evaluating these stories as worth telling.

The discussion of disnarration is also extended to consider plot and story time in films where disruption to both arguably provides a more satisfying, though unconventional story. Underpinning the discussion of each of the texts is an analysis of the linguistic strategies that convey the various unconventional narrative dimensions to understand their form as well as their function.

Chapter 1 *Introduction to Disnarration and the Unmentioned in Fact and Fiction* presents the overall aims and scope of this book. The structure of the book thereafter is organised with each chapter focusing on a specific genre of storytelling, that is, either a factual or fictional narrative to explore disnarration, narrative gaps, counterfactual scenarios etc. Discussions of each of the texts will also describe the lexico-grammatical structures and their function in creating these compelling storytelling strategies. It is hoped that an exploration of both literary and non-literary texts will offer further insights to contribute to a greater understanding of unconventional storytelling strategies at the intersection of narratology and stylistics.

Chapter 2 *Telling Stories* presents an overview of some of the key concepts in the study of narratives to situate the disnarrated within a broader context of narrative storytelling as a universal activity. A useful discussion of what is understood by the term "narrative" looks to prototypical characteristics and models in literature (Todorov 1977; Forster 1927) and (socio)linguistics (Labov and Waletzky 1967; Labov 1972) to understand their form and function. Central to the effectiveness of a successful narrative is the presence of Trouble with a capital 'T' (Bruner 1997; Burke 1945) which defines complication, conflict or disequilibrium to give the narrative the qualities of narrativity and tellability. The chapter describes Prince's disnarrated together with the extended work on narrative refusals, the nonnarratable and textual gaps. Also explored are the absences in the text generated through negation and hypothetical conditional structures that invite audiences to fill in gaps to make sense of the story. The chapter also discusses Possible Worlds Theory to situate parallel universes and counterfactual divergence (Dannenberg 2008) such as those triggered by forking paths (Borges 2000 [1944]) that lead to a network of plot possibilities (Bremond and Cancalon 1980) and 'what might have been' scenarios. The final section of the chapter argues that disnarrated narratives are unnatural narratives because they violate expectations of plot structure, temporality, narration and characterisation.

Chapter 3 *Disnarration and the Unmentioned in Fact: Oral Narratives of Personal Experience* presents the first of two chapters that examines disnarration in factual narratives. The chapter focuses on the disnarrated personal narratives produced by children on themes about danger of death and fight experiences as part of a wider study of personal narratives. Children produced personal narratives that were 'fully-formed' when analysed against Labov and Waletzky's (1967) narrative model but also narrated experiences recalling events that *nearly* or *almost* happened, or *could have happened* using conditional statements and negation. The explicit reference to events that do not happen are examined to understand why these types of personal narratives are told and concludes with an argument that disnarrated experiences are not only an important part of a child's repertoire of stories but also necessary for their socialisation.

Chapter 4 *Disnarration and the Unmentioned in Fact: News Stories* explores the presence of disnarration in factual narratives, specifically, news stories. The chapter begins with a discussion of news values (Bell 1991) to explore the function of news stories and which criteria make events newsworthy for the purpose of being printed and shared. As the concept of truth is a central requirement of news stories, the question of how disnarrated stories that report on what does not happen is raised as disnarration appears to undermine existing notions of newsworthiness. By applying a discourse analytic approach to news stories (Bednarek and Caple 2014) about *near miss* scenarios and events that could have happened but did not, the analysis explains the significance of disnarrated incidents in terms of the criteria of *NEGATIVITY* and *PERSONALISATION* (Bell 1991). Audiences are able to speculate on the possible and potentially devastating outcomes, however hypothetical and counterfactual, which contribute to determining the news agenda.

Chapter 5 *Disnarration and the Unmentioned in Fiction* examines three genres of fictional narratives for an exploration of disnarration, forking paths and counterfactual divergence as narratives strategies to tell compelling stories in a novel, short story and film. The three texts are: John Fowles's (1969) *The French Lieutenant's Woman*, analysed for disnarration and metafictive devices, such as the use of metalepsis for unusual and startling plot developments; Tobias Wolff's (1996) short story *Bullet in the Brain*, for insights on how disnarration communicated through a marked use of negation also offers insights into characterization; and the 2016 film *La La Land*, written and directed by Damien Chazelle, where the counterfactual ending generated in the imaginations of the protagonists and then disnarrated within moments, could never have happened. Analysis of all thee fictional narratives emphasise how plot options, disnarration and the creative use of negation reinforce the arguement that plot consequences are the result of protagonists having volition in their storyworld.

Chapter 5 *Final Thoughts* draws together the main findings dealing with disnarration and the unmentioned from discussions across the different genres of storytelling in Chapters 3–5 with a final commentary.

References

Bednarek, M., & Caple, H. (2014). Why Do News Values Matter? Towards a New Methodological Framework for Analysing News Discourse in Critical Discourse Analysis and Beyond. *Discourse and Society, 25*(2), 135–158.

Bell, A. (1991). *The Language of News Media*. Oxford: Blackwell.

Borges, J. L. (2000 [1944]). The Garden of Forking Paths. In *Collected Fictions* (Andrew Hurley, Trans., pp. 119–128). London: Penguin.

Bremond, C., & Cancalon, E. D. (1980). The Logic of Narrative Possibilities. *New Literary History, 11*(3), 387–411.

Bruner, J. (1997). Labov and Waletzky Thirty Years On. *Journal of Narrative and Life History, 7*(1–4), 61–68.

Burke, K. (1945). *A Grammar of Motives*. New York: Prentice Hall.

Dannenberg, H. P. (2008). *Coincidence and Counterfactuality: Plotting Time and Space in Narrative Fiction*. Lincoln and London: University of Nebraska Press.

Dannenberg, H. P. (2014). Gerald Prince and the Fascination of What Doesn't Happen. *Narrative, 22*(3), 304–311.

Forster, E. M. (1927). *Aspects of the Novel*. London: Edward Arnold.

Fowles, J. (1969). *The French Lieutenant's Woman*. London: Vintage.

Labov, W. (1972). *Language in the Inner City*. Philadelphia: University of Pennsylvania Press.

Labov, W., & Waletzky, J. (1967). Narrative Analysis: Oral Versions of Personal Experience. In J. Holm (Ed.), *Essays on the Verbal and Visual Arts* (pp. 12–44). Seattle: University of Washington Press.

Prince, G. (1988). The 'Disnarrated'. *Style, 22*(1), 1–8.

Todorov, T. (1977). *The Poetics of Prose*. Oxford: Blackwell.

Twain, M. (1924). *Mark Twain*'s *Autobiography* (Vol. 1). New York and London: Harper & Brothers.

Warhol, R. R. (2005). Neonarrative; Or, How to Render the Unnarratable in Realist Fiction and Contemporary Film. In J. Phelan & P. Rabinowitz (Eds.), *A Companion to Narrative Theory* (pp. 220–231). Oxford: Blackwell.

Warhol, R. (2007). Narrative Refusals and Generic Transformation in Austen and James: What Doesn't Happen in Northanger Abbey and Spoils of Poynton. *Henry James Review, 28*(3), 259–268.

Warhol, R. (2010). "What Might Have Been Is Not What Is": Dickens's Narrative Refusals. *Dickens Studies Annual, 41*, 45–60.

Wolff, T. (1996). Bullet in the Brain. In *The Night in Question* (pp. 200–206). London: Bloomsbury.

CHAPTER 2

Telling Stories

Abstract This chapter discusses what is understood by the term *narrative* by turning to well-known literary and linguistic models to examine prototypical features associated with the discourse of storytelling. A discussion of the purpose of telling stories as a social activity and a closer look at the characteristics of narratives, such as the importance of causation and the presence of Trouble with a capital 'T', will provide further insights to contextualise the aims of the book and highlight the important qualities of *narrativity* and *tellability*. The chapter goes on to describe the various forms of Prince's (1988) disnarration, before discussing narrative refusals and textual gaps as unconventional dimensions. As disnarration makes explicit reference to that which does not happen, it simultaneously conjures up 'what might have been' negated scenarios, so the concepts of possible worlds, counterfactual storytelling and forked paths that give rise to alternative plots paths are also outlined.

Keywords Narrative · Narrativity · Tellability · Disnarration · Narrative refusals · Negation · Negative uninformativeness · Textual gaps · Possible Worlds Theory · Counterfactual divergence

M. Lambrou, *Disnarration and the Unmentioned in Fact and Fiction*,
https://doi.org/10.1057/978-1-137-50778-5_2

Understanding Narrative

Storytelling in all its different forms is generally accepted as a universal activity that is practised across cultures (Miller and Moore 1989). At its most basic level, a narrative requires 'the presence of a story and a story-teller' (Scholes and Kellogg 1966: 4). The dynamic characterisation of a narrative is what Cobley (2014: 21–22) describes as humans having a propensity for organising experiences into narrative form, a consequence of language that 'not only "permits" narratives but practically makes them obligatory in the organization of human experience'. Narrativizing our past helps us to make sense of our existence and sense of self as through the narrative mode, we ascribe meaning to experiences in stories about human or humanlike intention. Branigan (1992: 3) describes narrative as 'a perceptual activity that organizes data into a special pattern which represents and explains experience' and contains 'cause-and effect chains of events' and an evaluation or 'judgement' of the events, while Popova (2015a: 494) claims that narratives are a form of social understanding 'an aspect of social cognition'. She explains that narrative 'is defined in terms of two of its crucial aspects, dynamic causal structure and participatory sense-making'. Many other theorists also foreground the socialising power of narratives in the construction of the self through the importance of remembering (Mandler et al. 1980; Shank and Abelson 1995; Miller 1995; Miller et al. 1996). Ryan (2007: 24, in Herman 2007) points out that while definitions of narrative are useful, 'none offers a complete and self-sufficient definition of narrative, because they depend too much on implicit elements' and goes on to offer a list of statements that could be incorporated as part of a definition of narrative:

> 'Narrative is about problem solving.
> Narrative is about conflict.
> Narrative is about interpersonal relations.
> Narrative is about human experience.
> Narrative is about the temporality of experience.'

In a discussion of storytelling as a literary form, Dancygier (2012: 4) takes a cognitive approach to understanding the relationship between language and literature and how stories construct meaning:

> Why do we enjoy stories? What's in it for us as a species? Could our culture exist without stories? Are they a mental construct, a linguistic construct or

> a cultural construct? Is there a difference between real stories and fictional stories?

Dancygier's questions presuppose the universal presence and importance of the narrative form across cultures and this emphasises the interdisciplinary nature of researching storytelling forms in language and literature, which are of interest not only to narratologists but also to linguists, literary theorists, anthropologists, philosophers, historians and psychologists etc. The oral storytelling tradition, for example, is thought to have emerged from conversational narratives and transitioned and developed into prose and literary texts, as literary models appear to contain the prototypical features of oral storytelling. Fludernik (1996: 94) explains how in late medieval and early modern literature:

> the epic and the verse romance, which are by generic definition prototypically third-person forms, have adopted some of the linguistic patterns from oral first-person stories, and how they have adopted an experiential (though vicarious) content along with the formal pattern.

Interestingly, the process goes both ways as the 'natural' narratives of conversation also adopt features of fictionality. Fludernik (2009: 59) argues that the 'essence' of narratives are more than sequences of events because they communicate 'anthropocentric experience – the experientiality which is inherent in human experience – and this means drawing on fixed patterns of behaviour as well as conveying thoughts and feelings, and depicting perceptions and reflections'. However, to render these states, the narrator has to rely on 'techniques of fiction'—the qualities that give the text fictionality—because even personal experiences constructed into narratives are merely representations of experientiality. In other words, all narrative forms are fictional. Ochs and Capps (2001: 33) recognise the 'blurring of boundaries between literary works and oral accounts of personal experiences' when highlighting the importance of tellability and audience response in both genres of storytelling. Literary and oral forms may be characterised by different features and researchers in these disciplines may have specific concerns that are distinct, or may overlap such as the theoretical models of stories that are borrowed and applied across disciplines.

The organisation of events to create a plot is central to all types of storytelling, whether factually derived through human experience as emplotment and grounded in human understanding of the world (mimesis) (Ricoeur 1980) or configured through imagination as fiction. Herman (2003: 165) argues that with the important process of transformation, narratives offer a 'tool for thinking' as 'stories provide important representational tools for humans – tools that facilitate a number of problem-solving activities'. The success of the narrative not only depends on the 'constitutive elements' and 'arrangement of the narrative but also on the context of the telling and to its "receiver"' (Prince 1982). Audiences are as significant as the text when describing the rhetorical importance of narratives. Storytelling then, is about 'somebody telling somebody else on some occasion and for some purposes that something happened' (Phelan 2017: ix) where it is characterised by the rhetorical aspects of performance and interaction with the audience playing an integral part in the narrative construction and communication. Dawson (2018) also offers a useful description of narrative as a communicative act that allows individuals make sense of the world:

> And so narrative is transformed by the cognitive revolution, from a noun to a verb. To narrativize is to make sense of the world, to narrativize is to emplot history, to narrativize is to invite empathy, to narrativize is to employ a 'natural' cognitive frame that will enable us to read any literary work as a narrative. It's what people do with narratives that makes them narrative, in the same way that what people do with artefacts constitutes popular culture. And in the same way that one's creativity guarantees individual selfhood, so does narrative: no longer a deliberate artful structure, but simply a way of thinking that guarantees our sense of identity as homo narrans.

In this book, the terms 'story' and 'narrative' are both used to describe a sequence of events with causation propelling events with an 'internal time sequence' that progresses in a 'chrono-logic' manner (Chatman 1990: 9). It does not differentiate between narrative discourse, which is how the sequence of events are presented and where time and order may not be linear. These terms are comparable to those offered by Russian Formalists who used the terms Fabula and Sjuzet, where Fabula refers to the basic story composed of a series of events, and where Sjuzet refers to how you tell the story. The Fabula corresponds with story, the basic unshaped story material which comprises event, characters and setting, and plot and Sjuzhet corresponds with the narrative discourse and representation of the story. This is a much more complex discussion and so for the purposes of this book, both story and narrative are used to describe a sequence of temporally ordered events that communicate that something has happened to someone or something, as exemplified by the narrative models in the next section.

Narrative Models

A narrative at its simplest description is 'based on cause-and-effect relationships that are applied to sequences of events' (Fludernik 2009: 2). The following examples of well-known literary and linguistic models of narrative provide an understanding of the prototypical internal structure while exemplifying the functional and tellable characteristics of this genre of storytelling.

Todorov's Narrative Model

The French-Bulgarian formalist Tzvetan Todorov (1977) proposed a model that can be applied to film texts that focuses on the organizing principle of narratives where events are linked through common factors that 'makes narrative possible and yields us its very definition' (Todorov 1977: 233). Narratives develop through five distinct stages with *equilibrium* at the start sharply contrasting with the disruption that follows. The chain of causality leads to narrative transformation as a consequence of *disequilibrium* before returning to *equilibrium* as the narrative develops:

I. A state of equilibrium at the outset
II. Some kind of disruption to the equilibrium = *disequilibrium*
III. Some kind of recognition that the disruption has taken place
IV. Some kind of attempt to repair the disruption
V. Restoration of equilibrium—but a new state of normal and stability.

Todorov's concept of *disequilibrium* is a consequence of disruption or crisis and as normality is regained, characters and situations are transformed in the process. However, the resulting new state of normality will differ from the state of affairs at the start of the narrative and before the crisis because a transformation has taken place. Unlike the linear structure of personal narratives and fiction, Todorov's narrative structure is circular and can be applied to the numerous and ongoing life experiences over time, each with their own patterns of transformation and each returning to a new state of equilibrium only to be to be disrupted again. News stories that are ongoing or dialogic, that is connected historically or over time by a series of similar events, may experience narrative transformation when embedded as part of a larger narrative composed of a series of smaller stories each narrating their own crisis.

Forster's Narrative Model

A well-known literary model of narrative that exemplifies the importance of making causality explicit to create plot and narrativity was proposed by the novelist and literary theorist E. M. Forster (1927). Foster's example of *The King died* demonstrates how three conditions of *temporality*, *causation* and *human interest* produce a minimal narrative by presenting three sets of sentences, a. b. and c., where each is progressively modified:

a. The King died. The Queen died
b. The King died and then the Queen died
c. The King died and then the Queen died of grief.

Forster argued that the two sentences in example *a.* provide factual information about two separate events; the absence of any conjunctions suggests that the two events are unrelated although readers are likely to infer intuitively that the sentences are related because King and Queen belong to the same semantic field. (Compare this with for example, *The King died. The dog died* which is semantically unrelated.) In example b. removing the full stop to create a single sentence connected by the addition of two conjunctions creates a temporal sequence of events that readers will see as being connected. Specifically, the coordinating conjunction *and* functions as an additive while the conjunction *then* functions as a temporal conjunction so readers can infer a chronological order where the King died before the Queen. As the conjunction *then* also functions as a causal conjunction, readers may also infer that the King's death caused the Queen to die. Here is an example of a minimal narrative with the important criteria of temporality and causation. By adding the prepositional phrase *of grief* in example *c.* the cause of the Queen's death is then made explicit and tells readers not only *what happened?* but *why?* to provide the plot. The important condition of human interest is now present to make the narrative tellable (and newsworthy if published) and in this way, fulfils expectations of a satisfying story. Without human interest there is no narrative 'for it is only in relation to a plan conceived by man that events gain meaning and can be organized into a structured temporal sequence' (Bremond and Cancalon 1980: 390).

Labov and Waletzky's Model of Narrative Schemas

One of the most influential models of narrative structure was developed by the sociolinguists Labov and Waletzky (1967) who set out to research variation in the speech of black and Hispanic communities in New York. In their ground breaking study, Labov and Waletzky asked informants to tell them about their personal experiences as a way to elicit large units of data for their investigation into linguistic variation (specifically, non-standard varieties). The topics for the personal experiences were based on fights and danger of death stories, which were important as it was thought that the more emotional the experience, the less likely it was that the informants would monitor their speech, causing a "style-shift" to the vernacular. This strategy would help to minimise the methodological problem of the Observer's Paradox (Labov 1972: 209) where 'the aim of linguistic research in the community must be to find out how people talk when they are not being systematically observed; yet we can only obtain these data by systematic observation'. Labov and Waletzky's groundbreaking methodology meant that they were able to collect the closest to natural and spontaneous speech possible in an interview setting.

A close analysis of the elicited personal narratives revealed common patterns in the internal structure of the stories in how they begin, progress, are evaluated and end, leading Labov and Waletzky to propose an analytical framework of narrative based on the idea of story schemas. They concluded that personal narratives are composed of six sections or schemas described as the ***abstract***, ***orientation***, ***complicating action***, ***evaluation***, ***resolution*** and ***coda*** that differ lexico-grammatically and functionally and are organised in a logical, temporal sequence—see Table 2.1.

Labov defined a minimal narrative as 'a sequence of two clauses which are temporally ordered' (1972: 360) and provide 'one method of recapitulating past experience by matching a verbal sequence of clauses to the sequence of events which...actually occurred' (pp. 359–360). A minimal narrative must not only be based on real events experienced by the

Table 2.1 Labov and Waletzky's (1967) model of narrative

Abstract	Signals the start of the narrative
Orientation	Provides the 'who?', 'what?', 'where?' and 'when?' of the narrative
Complicating action	Provides the sequence of events; the 'what happened' of the story
Evaluation	Provides the narrator's evaluation of the events; the 'so what?' of the narrative
Resolution	provides the final part of the complicating action; the 'what finally happened?' of the story
Coda	Signals the end of the story and may be a generalised statement or in the form of a moral or a lesson

narrator (and therefore excludes vicarious experiences) but they must also be temporally ordered. To illustrate, consider the two examples below where a. is a minimal narrative but b. is not:

a. Carl unlocked the door and then entered the building
b. Carl entered the building after he unlocked the door

In example a. the coordinating conjunction ***and*** connects the two events while ***then*** provides the temporal juncture in the experience. When the events are reversed in example b. the coordinating conjunction is lost as the order of the events are flipped so it is no longer a narrative in Labov and Waletzky's definition. As they explain, the ***complicating action*** contains the actual events in the sequence in which they occurred, that is, 'this happened… then this happened' and it is here where you find the crisis or high point. In later work, Labov (1972) revised details of the ***evaluation*** schema, which can often describe narrative clauses in an irrealis mood to communicate the important '***so what?***' of how the narrator feels about their experience. Irrealis clauses function by evaluating events that occurred with those that did not i.e. through the use of comparators (negation, modality, hypothetical clauses etc.) to generate alternative outcomes. Through a range of ***internal*** and ***external*** linguistic markers, ***evaluation*** is not always presented as a complete section after the ***complication action*** but could be embedded at any stage of the narrative as 'waves of evaluation' woven into the story. Narratives are expected to have a ***point*** that conveys not just what the story is about but the purpose for its telling and evaluative strategies together with the events in the ***complicating action*** communicate this.

Trouble with a Capital 'T'

Central to our understanding of narrative form and function is the theme of conflict or crisis to drive the plot, transform experiences and provide the necessary quality of tellability. Trouble in some form is expected as the narrative models proposed by Todorov, Labov and Waletzky, and to some extent, Foster outlined in the previous section show. News stories are also expected to report the news value of *NEGATIVITY* (Bell 1991) to guarantee newsworthiness for publication/reporting, especially where events involve the violation of an expected rule of behaviour.

One of the criticisms of Labov and Waletzky's data is that the theme of conflict as the basis for eliciting personal experiences not only guarantees a narrative structure with a 'high point' in the *complicating action* but also promises tellability. By asking informants for experiences about danger of death and fight experiences, it follows that the more dangerous the experience, the more tellable the story is likely to be, as 'Trouble' with a capital 'T' defines complication (Bruner 1997). As Bruner (1997: 63) explains:

> Labov and Waletzky take Trouble so much for granted as the heart of complication that they even gathered their corpus of narratives so as to guarantee its presence. Recall that they asked their subjects to tell about a time when their lives were endangered - the ultimate trouble! And, of course, it's virtually in the structure of narrative that if a story contains a troubled complication, it requires some explication about how things were before it got that way - that is, an orientation, telling how things were before the trouble erupted.

The concept of 'Trouble' builds on the earlier work of Burke (1945) and his 'dramatist Pentad' and no doubt provides the necessary factor that gives a narrative its narrativity. According to Prince (1982: 147), 'depicting a conflict of some kind should function better narratively than one depicting no conflict at all' and to illustrate this point, he compares two examples of minimal narratives: 'The cat sat on the mat' and 'The cat sat on the dog's mat' suggesting that the latter 'may be the beginning of a good story'. The justification for narrating any story, or the most reportable event, whether factual or fictional may be based on the level of 'Trouble', which guarantees the necessary success and narrativity of the story.

Narrativity

The earlier narrative models outlined above describe texts with temporally ordered sequences of events with causality but this suggests that stories communicating atemporal plots that subvert the 'chrono-logic' trajectory (Chatman 1990: 9) and goals of the story are non-narratives. In addition to a coherent structure, narratives must also possess the abstract condition of narrativity or narrativehood, which Prince (2005: 387) defines as:

> the quality of being narrative, the set of properties characterising narratives and distinguishing them from non-narratives' […] It also designates the set of optional features that make narrative more prototypically narrative-like, more immediately identified, processed, and interpreted as narratives.

Narrativity, according to Prince (1982: 147) is integral to the context and dynamic of its telling as what is 'highly narrative for you may not be highly narrative for me'. A useful way of visualising the condition of narrativity is not as something that is binary, where it is either present or absent but as a 'fuzzy set allowing varying degrees of membership' (Herman 2007: 29) with prototypical features that makes the text type recognizable as a narrative. Herman (2007) imagines a set of concentric circles with the inner circle presenting the prototype with each subsequent outer circle presenting broader conditions and marginal cases with less narrativity. Herman organizes the conditions of narrativity into three semantic dimensions—Spatial, Temporal and Mental—one formal dimension and one pragmatic dimension, and offers a 'tool-kit for do-it-yourself' definitions to be able to answer the question "is this text a narrative?". (See Herman 2007: 29–30 for the detailed list of conditions and dimensions.) So, there appear to be degrees of narrativity corresponding with degrees of telling a better story where some narratives are more narrative than others. Abbott (2008: 25) also discusses the concept of degrees of narrativity by offering the following examples of minimal narratives to illustrate this point:

(a) She ate lunch.
(b) She ate lunch. Then she drove her car to work.
(c) Brooding, she ate lunch. Then she drove her car to work.

Readers are likely to agree that (c) offers the most narrativity as the word 'brooding' contributes to increasing narrativity as it 'is more common to narrative than it is to ordinary discourse. Or it may be because the word gives depth to the character (she has a mind and there is something troubling it)' (Abbott 2008: 25). Similar to Prince's point that narrativity is subjective, Abbott also suggests that narrativity 'has so much to do with subjective human response' (p. 25). Ryan (2005: 347) makes the distinction between 'being a narrative' and 'possessing narrativity' where narrativity describes the narrativeness of a narrative though this depends on how well the narrative is received, processed and interpreted. Narrativity, the quality of being a narrative, is not only found within the set of properties that characterise a narrative but has to do with how readily a text can be interpreted as a narrative and fulfil a reader's expectations of narrativeness. The emotional and cognitive effect of a good story is fundamental to narrativity, which according to Sternberg (2010: 642) is based on 'the play of suspense/ curiosity /surprise between represented and communicative time'. Readerly effect is also a factor in Popova's (2015a: 496) definition as narrativity which 'involves the shaping of causality by the very process of narration' as readers piece together the events for their understanding. Popova proposes a model of how stories take place as a cognitive process based on 'elements of perceived causality among the events that a narrative reports and a reader's enaction of a specific narratorial viewpoint relating to those events' (p. 494). Narratives become dynamic in the act of narrative reconstruction which occurs in the interaction between minds when readers 'engage with and enact their content'. Popova takes the work of the experimental psychologist Albert Michotte (1963 [1946]) on perceptual causality as the basis for her study, where causality is perceived rather than inferred, the reason being that causality is intentional because human actions are intentional and goal orientated. (In this definition, perceptual causality is based on movement and factors such as speed, direction and size. See also Popova [2015b].)

Tellability

The discussion of narrative structure and function and the condition of narrativity cannot be separated from another important feature of stories—tellability. Tellability is what makes a story worth telling in the first place so there must be some kind of intrinsic interest in the *so what?* point of the story. Bruner (1991) argues that without tellability there can be no narrativity as narrativity and tellability are entwined and the presence of one entails the presence of the other. Herman (2002: 100), however, reminds us that narratologists differentiate between the two in that 'whereas both predicates are scalar, tellability attaches to configurations of facts and narrativity to sequences representing configurations of facts'. Other factors such as 'the entertainment value, the exceptional nature of the events narrated, and the story's moral' (Fludernik 2009: 48) are also important for tellability as is the theme of Trouble with a capital 'T' discussed above.

Tellability is a requirement in virtually all types of storytelling activities where there is a recipient involved. In conversation analysis, stories need to fulfil listener expectations as well as justify the speaker role and extended turn as 'the sheer telling of a story is something in which one makes a claim for its tellability' (Sacks 1992: 12). In media discourses, such as news broadcasts, publications and online reporting of local, national and global events, tellable events must fulfil specific news values and the criteria of newsworthiness although these may be culturally biased. (See Chapter 4: *Disnarration and the Unmentioned in Fact: News Stories.*) In naturally occurring narratives, such as oral narratives of personal experiences, tellability is expressed through a range of linguistic devices to communicate internal and external evaluation. The evaluative devices include intensifiers, comparators, correlatives and explicatives and the more evaluation embedded in the personal narrative there are, the more explicit and enhanced the *so what?* point of the story is. In 'Further steps in narrative analysis', Labov (1997: 407), defined a reportable event as 'one that justifies the automatic reassignment of speaker role to the narrator' so 'The more reportable the most reportable event of a narrative, the greater justification for the automatic reassignment of speaker role to the narrator'. Narratives, therefore, should fulfil claims of tellability as '[A] person tells or listens to a story because the story has a content of some intrinsic interest. The content that bears this interest value is [...] the point' (Wilensky 1983: 583). Similar to narrativity, the tellability or reportability factor can be considered as scalar as the success of the story depends on the audience's judgement and evaluation of the narrative.

THE UNNARRATABLE, NONNARRATABLE AND THE DISNARRATED

The chapter has so far discussed some of the key concepts for understanding narrative based on conventional features and expectations and more abstract concepts to provide a context for an exploration of the disnarrated and the unmentioned. This section turns to the unconventional narrative strategies outlined in the Introduction that are central to the aims of the book before being applied to a range of narrative texts across Chapters 3–5.

One of the most imaginative contributions to the study of narrative was proposed by the narratologist Gerald Prince (1988) in an article published in *Style* entitled 'The Disnarrated'. Prince describes the phenomenon of what does not happen in narratives and considers how this is expressed by categorising what is not represented in fiction. Prince refers to them as the *unnarratable* and *nonnarratable* and explains there are three types of categories of text that remain unmentioned. The first refers to actions and experiences that may seem mundane and/or 'cannot be narrated or is not worth narrating' (p. 1) and gives the example of omitting details of tying up one's shoelace. He also points out that in terms of defamiliarization, it can be effective to include the ordinary and the uneventful as this can give the work its force. Prince also describes the *unnarratable* or *nonnarratable* as the intentional lacuna or ellipses in the text including those narrated by the narrator who explicitly states what they will not say. Prince's third category, the *disnarrated* (from the French 'dénarré) 'covers all the events that *do not* happen but, nonetheless, are referred to (in a negative or hypothetical mode) by the narrative text' (p. 2). To summarise, Prince's (1988) *unnarratable* and *nonnarratable* categories describe:

i. events that cannot be narrated or are not worth narrating
ii. intentional gaps or ellipses rhythm, characterisation or for invoking surprise or suspense etc.
iii. events that do not happen but nonetheless are referred to in a negative or hypothetical way in the narrative (the *disnarrated*)

The distinction between the first two categories and the third is that the unnarratable describes events that cannot be narrated or are not worth narrating and so express something that is marked as explicitly not there.

Disnarration, on the other hand, is when a narrator explicitly states that something did not happen. An example of the unnarratable is the underdeveloped or minor characters in realist fiction (Mosher 1993), and what Chatman (1978: 139) describes as the 'walk-ons' or 'extras' such as the hordes of soldiers, who although part of the setting, are not regarded as characters and are too insignificant to name. This may also be the case with objects not named or parts of ellipted speech which are not worth stating explicitly. The *unnarratable* as a dimension storytelling is extended further in Warhol's (2005, 2010, 2013) work on Victorian Fiction such as the works of Charles Dickens, George Eliot and Henry James. Warhol (2010: 46) examines gaps in the novels and focused on a particular novelistic style she describes as *narrative refusals* defined as 'Direct narratorial references to some of the specifics or *what might have been and yet is not*'. Warhol (2010: 46) explains that *narrative refusals* are subject to 'distinctive markers of a genre' such as nation, period, and audience, and these markers can all affect and limit narratability and what can and cannot be narrated:

> Every time a narrator elides, represses, supresses, passes over, leaves out or ignores some action, utterance, feeling or impression that implicitly occurs in the storyworld, that gap or lacuna represents an element that is unnarratable for that genre in that era.

Warhol (2005, 2010, 2013) offers a useful taxonomy of the *unnarratable* or narrative refusals in relation to what is narratable, which are subdivided into four categories to explain their specific function:

i. *Subnarratable* is what need not be told because it is too boring
ii. *Supranarratable* is what cannot be told because it is ineffable or inexpressible
iii. *Antinarratable* is what should not be told because of trauma or taboo
iv. *Paranarratable* is what would not (yet) be told because of literary convention

To explain, the *subnarratable* would exclude mundane events that would not necessarily enhance the narrativity and tellability of the play because they are unremarkable, similar to Prince's (1988) description of the *nonnarratable*. The *supranarratable* describes something that cannot be told because the emotion, trauma or horror, for example, are best left unsaid resulting in the audience needing to fill in any gaps. The third category, the *antinarratable*, refers to what remains unspoken because it is bound by cultural and historical conventions. In other words, anything transgressing social laws and taboos would be deemed as unacceptable even in realist Victorian novels where themes of poverty, trauma and abuse are present. An example of the antinarratable would be the omission of sexual activities and mention of bodily functions. The *paranarratable* is more complex as it is more strictly bound to the literary genre and conventions of its time and refers to plot turns that would not be taken or would be thought improbable. Warhol explains that female protagonists either marry or die in Victorian novels and characters who remain unmarried and live would not be remarked upon. The characters and plots in the storyworld, it would seem, are expected to be representative and mimetic of the real discourse-world. *Narrative refusals* as marked dimensions of storytelling are also indicative of an author's style and their distinctive way of expressing and withholding aspects of the story. To give an example, Jane Austen's use of irony in *Northanger Abbey* (1817) with her 'in-your-face flouting of romance conventions could well have played a role in publishers' reluctance to bring the novel out' (Warhol 2007: 260). Warhol explains that the categories of narrative refusals are not an exhaustive description of the gaps arising from the unnarratable. In a critique of this work, Rosaler (2016: 10) points out that the list of *narrative refusals* does not account for the 'exploitation of narrative gaps for psychological mimesis, nor does it address narrative gaps' potential uses in the creation of narrative games or the communication of inexplicit plot lines', citing the omissions in *Vanity Fair* (1848). The argument here is that Thackeray deliberately sets out to communicate a personal evaluation of Becky Sharp's motives by fashioning a particular 'narrative tone'.

The final category of the *nonnarrated* and the *disnarrated* is of greatest interest as a dimension of narrative storytelling in this book and is explored across a range of factual and fictional stories for their pervasiveness. Disnarration, according to Prince's (1988: 2) can be expressed by the narration, narrator or character but is constructed through:

> alethic expressions of impossibility or unrealized possibility, deontic expressions of observed prohibition, epistemic expressions of ignorance, ontologic expressions of nonexistence, purely imagined worlds, desired worlds, or intended worlds, unfulfilled expectations, unwarranted beliefs, failed

> attempts, crushed hopes, suppositions and false calculations, errors and lies, and so forth.

In later work, Prince (2003: 22) expanded his definition of disnarration by explaining it is 'The elements in a narrative that explicitly consider and refer to what does not take place ("X didn't happen"; "Y could have happened but didn't")'. In terms of lexico-grammatical features, disnarration is expressed through comparators such as negation, modality and hypothetical clauses and while some devices are explicitly stated, others rely on the reader's ability to infer and interpret what does not happen. This mode of storytelling can be found across a range of text types including conversational narratives, personal narratives, literary, historical and film narratives, and news media stories etc., to provide a thought-provoking experience of storytelling where the rhetorical function across all genres appear to overlap (as the analysis of a range of narrative genres later in the book will show). Disnarration as a mode of storytelling might prompt the *what is the point of disnarration*? question as narrativity and tellability linked to the presence of causality and transformation are important conditions of a narrative yet disnarration describes something that does not happen, events referred to but not explicitly described, and events that might have happened but did not. One answer is to consider what disnarration does as a plot device rather than what it does not. Disnarration can create suspense by presenting possible and false solutions in contrast with the correct and inevitable one, in for example, detective fiction. It can also slow down the plot as other, less conventional outcomes and pathways are invoked to intentionally distract the audience. Another answer is that through disnarration, Prince was able to theorize the imaginary as significant because he:

> directs our attention to the issue of how vital the hypothetical in fact is in its dynamic and contrastive interaction with events which are deemed to "really happen" in a narrative world, and he shows that such questions are not only ontologically complex but rhetorically significant in a variety of ways. (Dannenberg 2014: 307)

Disnarration can also provide insights into characters in their storyworld, as their hopes, wishes and desires of what might have been are revealed. In this way characters are presented as conscious beings despite their fictional setting, and their interior thoughts may help readers relate better to their situations and motivations. Moreover, a greater understanding and (interpretation of motives) may contribute to their development as flat or round characters (Forster 1927: 75–78) where round characters are 'more highly organized' and 'capable of surprising in a convincing way'. Prince (1988) quotes a passage from *Bel-Ami* to illustrate the protagonist's hopes of marrying well and in so doing represents the character's mind as real or as Dannenberg (2014: 307) explains 'the disnarrated allows the depiction of characters as living in an uncertain world of possible events – a world more like the one we inhabit'. The narrator's description of what does not happen in place of what does is also used effectively in the opening chapter of Jane Austen's *Northanger Abbey* where Catherine Morland, the heroine of the novel, is introduced:

> She had reached the age of seventeen, without having seen one amiable youth who could call forth her sensibility, without having inspired one real passion, and without having excited even any admiration… There was not one lord in the neighbourhood; no — not even a baronet. There was not one family among their acquaintance who had reared and supported a boy accidentally found at their door — not one young man whose origin was unknown. Her father had no ward, and the squire of the parish no children. (Austen 2003: 4)

In this excerpt, readers are told unambiguously that the men who are absent are in fact the most suitable for the heroine in comparison to the youths who are actually present in her surroundings but are not mentioned (Warhol 2007). Here, disnarration is conveyed through the use of negation with the emphatic 'without' delivered with irony and through the rhetorical device of the 'list of three' to convey what is absent. The foregrounded use of 'not' (repeated four times) and 'no' (repeated three times) functions to disrupt readers' expectations based on their schematic knowledge of this genre of novel leaving readers in no doubt as to the narrator's opinion on the matter of Catherine's marriage prospects. This is a example of 'negative uninformativeness' (Leech 1983) discussed in greater detail in the following paragraphs.

Unlike characters narrated in the third person, first person I-narrators are often aware of living in an uncertain world as in the *Twilight* stories (Meyer 2006) where Bella Swan describes the improbable situation she finds herself in. The opening paragraphs shows her trying to make sense of her circumstances through her thought presentation:

> I'D NEVER GIVEN MUCH THOUGHT TO HOW I WOULD DIE […] but even if I had, I would not have imagined it like this […]
>
> I knew that if I'd never gone to Forks, I wouldn't be facing death now. (p. 1)

The *if+would* conditional structures suggest there may have been other choices or options Bella could have taken for an alternative outcome at this point in her story, also emphasised by the use of negation—'would not' and 'never'. As this excerpt is narrated at the very beginning of the novel, audiences have no prior knowledge of events that have happened and why she is facing death or why the reference to Forks is significant. Moreover, audiences have no knowledge of the unnamed I-narrator so these linguistic devices provide interesting hooks to draw the reader in.

How does negation work in terms of forcing the reader to notice absences or non-existent versions of the world? Jeffries (2010: 107) defines negating as a generic term to refer to 'broader than the simple negating of a verb' and includes elements such as *lack, absence, dearth, scarcity* (nouns); *fail, omit, refuse* (verbs); *none, no one, nobody, nothing* (pronouns); *absent, scarce* (adjectives) as well as the obvious *no* and *not.* As Jeffries (2010) explains, audiences tend to construct an ideal version of the world as in the example *He does not love me* or to enhance a narrative as in *He didn't reach the bridge on time.* Both examples presuppose an ideal or preferred state of affairs so the negated version describes a marked unsatisfactory lack of some kind and alerts people to it. Further examples of negation conveying the opposite of the ideal scenario is illustrated in *The Awakening* (Chopin 1993 [1899]) to poignantly express Edna's feelings about Robert's continuing absence:

> Robert did not come that day. She was keenly disappointed. He did not come the following day, nor the next. (p. 146)

The emphatic description of Robert's absence highlights an unfulfilled expectation and reveals Edna's idealised version of her hopes which are unrealized. Leech (1983: 101) in a discussion of Grice's (1975) conversational maxims proposed a sub-maxim to explain negation called *negative uninformativeness* which he saw as flouting the maxim of quantity. *Negative uninformativeness* functions because positive versions are generally expected to carry greater informativity so 'the choice of a negative construction must signal a particular exception to the rule and draw attention to the specific informativity of the negative construction' (Giovanelli 2013: 126). In cognitive terms, negation is more difficult to process because it generates an implicature or a further richer meaning that has to be inferred and this in turn can give rise to stylistic effects. Thus, unrealized events are more informative than a positive statement because they are 'in pragmatic terms, denials of positive propositions which are in some sense 'present in the context' (Leech 1983: 101). The positive statement is therefore the expectation or norm and becomes noticeably marked when the negative statement is narrated. The excerpt from *The Versions of Us* (Barnett 2015) illustrates negative uninformativeness as readers are told of Jim's forgotten memories of his children when the expectation is that these are memories one should remember:

> Jim doesn't remember many of these moments – the ebb and flow of everyday life with a small child – from Jennifer and Daniel's childhood. (p. 314)

Readers are alerted to the proposition that Jim should have remembered these memories as the preferred version of himself and his awareness of this fact is expressed further in the following sentences where his reflections are conveyed with the reporting verbs *realise* ('He had come to *realise*...') and *wonders* ('He wonders now how Eva managed it...'). (An analysis of Wolff's (1996) *Bullet in the Brain* short story that discusses disnarration in relation to memories that are marked as not remembered is presented in Chapter 5.) Prince (1992: 33) claimed that negation is not disnarration but explained this point refers to merely descriptive actions that do not add to the narrative plot or the diegesis, to communicate 'a possibility that remains unrealized'. He offered two examples of this type of description to exemplify his point: 'Warren did not close the door' and 'Elizabeth did not answer'. These differ conceptually from the negation describing Jim's memories because Prince's examples could have happened, whereas Jim's forgotten memories did not, so 'the content of a dream, the components of a hallucination or delirium, can be disnarrated only if they are given as real possibilities in the relevant diegesis' (Prince (1992: 34).

In Hardy's *Tess of the D'Urbervilles* (1891) the nature of Tess's assault by Alec d'Urberville has been debated because the description is ambiguous and made more so by Hardy's changes to the fifth edition of the novel making it difficult to ascertain whether it was rape or seduction.

However, a close reading of the text suggests a darker understanding of events as Davis (1997: 223) argues:

> the assault upon Tess begins with an absence of verbal communication between Tess and Alec. Tess does not respond to Alec's address, and the narrator later adds that "silence ruled everywhere around"... The rape of Tess actually begins with the passage that describes Tess's sleep and her lack of verbal response-the passage, in short, that establishes her lack of consent to Alec's advances.

Tess's lack of response as a form of negation confirms that rape took place and for alert Victorian readers, these details would have 'confirmed rather than introduced the idea of rape'. The deliberate absence of such violent content is a category of the *antinarratable* because it is too traumatic to be told.

The expression of negation and hypothetical events in literature was also identified as a storytelling strategy by earlier theorists including the sociolinguists Labov and Waletzky (1967) who found examples of comparators in oral narratives of personal experiences. Unrealized events were compared with realized ones and functioned to express what could have happened: the use of negative sentences 'provide a way of evaluating events by placing them against a background of other events which might have happened, but did not' (Labov 1972: 381). The literary and linguistic theorist Viktor Shklovsky (1991 [1925]) describes the feature of negative parallelism and negative (or hypothetical) comparison in poetic imagery as a device that makes readers look afresh at the text because it purposely stands out, which suggests that it functions as a foregrounding device (Mukařovsky 1964 [1932]) giving the text tellability and narrativity. As a storytelling dimension, Karttunen (2008: 419) describes disnarration as being 'inconveniently wide [...] ranging from explicit denials to lengthy passages of imagined or otherwise hypothetical events'. Whatever the scope and form, disnarration has influenced the work of other narratologists who have developed related areas of the hypothetical and the *nonnarrated* in narrative theory, most notably, Warhol (2005, 2010, 2013) and her work on *narrative refusals* in Victorian realist novels, discussed in this chapter; Ryan (1991, 2013) and her work on possible worlds; and Dannenberg's (2008) on the counterfactual in fiction.

The Unmentioned: Textual Gaps

In his discussion of the disnarrated, Prince (1988) identifies a specific category of the *nonnarratable* to refer to omissions expressed as intentional gaps or ellipses that are used to invoke surprise or suspense. Wilson (2000: 18) defines ellipses as 'Structural gaps that can be related to (a) omitted elements recoverable from the linguistic context, (b) other potential syntactic forms, (c) the situational context' and states that what is missing is contextually recoverable. Narrative gaps are also defined as 'a specific piece of information, either a participant in an event or an entire proposition (event plus participants), that is noticeably missing or delayed in the narrative discourse' (Hardy 2005: 364). In both definitions, a gap is part of the narration because it communicates something by its very absence by drawing attention to itself although Toolan (2001) points out some ellipses are preferred as readers do not need to know every dull detail of what a character says or does. Hardy (2005) questions whether there is a 'stylistics of gaps' where 'gapping patterns' may characterise the style of particular authors. Authorial style is central to Montoro's (2018) corpus stylistic analysis of Henry Green's (1929) novel *Living* which identifies 'creative absences' in Green's 'unorthodox' use of determiners (indefinite article, definite article and possessives) in noun phrases. Montoro argues that in Green's work, creative absences 'reflect not so much the intricacies of the language system but the author's penchant for experimentation' (p. 283). Of stylistic interest is the fact that Green does not omit every instance of a determiner so his choices appear to be random and the effect, unexpected. An example is given below where in Standard English the definite article *the* would be present for a grammatical structure but is deliberately left out (with the null sign Ø denoting the omission):

> In Ø morning Mr Dupret came to Ø office. Soon Mr Archer came into his office.
>
> He said good-morning sir and said how was the Chief and Mr Dupret said they hoped to move him into Ø country tomorrow afternoon. (Green 1929: 79)

In a study of Joyce's (1914) *Dubliners*, Mosher (1993) found examples of gaps in the form of vague language that omit referents in characters' speech and thought, as well as gaps in suppressed thoughts that he claims contributes to characterisation. Mosher describes the use of gaps in terms of Prince's (1988) *nonnarrated*, that is, what cannot be narrated or is not worth narrating. Mosher (1993: 407) also identified examples of the disnarrated with words that 'could/should have been', acts that 'could/should have been performed' and states that 'could/should have existed but do not', as well as 'objects that could/should have been produced'. Hardy (2005: 366) categories the vague language in Flannery O'Conner's short stories that convey the *nonnarrated* as the 'announced gap' where the indefinite pronoun word 'something' is stated but not retrospectively filled, as shown in the examples 1–3 below. (Other types of gaps are attenuated announced gaps, ellipses, indeterminacies, and unannounced narrative gaps. See Hardy 2003):

1. He came back almost at once, plugging *something* into his ear
2. He lifted the gun to his eye and leaned forward. *Something* slipped beneath him and he slid on his heels
3. *Something* forced Mr Head from behind the trash box and forward, but only at a creeping pace.

In these examples, the announced gaps expressed through the use of the indefinite pronoun *something* could be the result of limited knowledge of the focalizer or narrator. Readers will rely on their schematic knowledge to help them to fill in the detail which may be effortless as in the hearing aid in 1. or requiring greater effort in examples 2. and 3. Because of how these gaps function, they act as a foregrounding device and the reader is made to notice what is not there.

The presence of ellipses in the form of temporal discontinuity where there is a jump from one scene to another could be said to function as the *subnarratable* (Warhol 2005) because a description of what occurred in between does not add to plot or is simply too dull to narrate. This type of ellipsis is what Prince (1988) describes as intentional gaps. For readers who are left to make interpretations to fill in the missing parts of the text, they are required to draw on various linguistic, schematic and cultural resources which can be challenging (Spolsky 2005). Simpson and Canning (2014: 292) explain that:

> By not narrating, the author creates a disjunction in the narrative and it is this gap that offers an extra layer of meaning. Although narrative gaps are 'non-narrated' events in the strict sense, they can be presupposed to have

occurred and can be 'filled in' retrospectively because the lacuna is marked in some way.

According to Iser (1978: 39) gaps are present in all narratives as breaks that 'cause indeterminacy' and it is through these that 'scenes and characters [come] to life'. Textual gaps can appear as bigger absences beyond word, clause, sentence and even paragraph levels as exemplified by Laurence Sterne's complex metafictional narrative *The Life and Opinions of Tristram Shandy, Gentleman* (1996 [1759]). Described as a modernist novel because of its experimental and self-conscious style that draws attention to its playfulness and linguistic and structural originality, the metafictive techniques 'not only examine the fundamental structures of narrative fiction, they also explore the possible fictionality of the world outside the literary fictional text' (Waugh 1984: 2). In *Tristram Shandy*, readers are confronted with incomplete texts filled with asterisks that convey a range of ***narrative refusals***. The example below of the ***anti-narratable*** shows the narrator failing to finish a sentence 'on grounds of decorum' in response to the gossip surrounding 'the accidental circumcision at the drop of a faulty window sash, when he was five years old':

> ...in a week's time, or less, it was in every body's mouth,
> *That poor Master Shandy* * * * *
> * * * *entirely.*
> (cited in Wilson 2000: 198)

Readers are expected to work at filling in the gaps which may result in creating meanings that differ for each reader. It can therefore be argued that meaning 'depends on the reader's creative engagement with the text, which in turn is enabled by moments of indeterminacy that allow the reader the space to do the work' (Abbott 2013: 108). Sometimes audiences cannot fill in gaps and 'cry out for authorial assistance', a concept Abbott (2013) calls 'egregious gaps'. Egregious gaps come in different forms but all share 'the capacity to call up immense inferential energy' (p. 112) and demands 'the most intense cognitive workout because how it is filled can have consequences for one's reading of the entire text' (p. 114). For example, readers are never told Iago's motives or what happened in the Marabar Caves or whether Heathcliff murdered Hindley Earnshaw. Audiences will nevertheless attempt to find an answer and this may affect their overall understanding or enjoyment of the text.

In *Tristram Shandy*, narrative gaps in the form of whole paragraphs being left blank and pages displayed in black are some of the other ways gaps are communicated. There is an example of the *supranarratable*—what cannot be told because it is inexpressible—when a whole page is left blank as Shandy is unable to describe the lustful widow Wadham, with whom his uncle Toby has fallen in love with. Shandy invites readers to 'call for pen and ink...to put [their] fancy in it' (p. 38) and fill in the gap with their own imagination. Other significant gaps include the infamous missing Chapter 24 in Volume 4 that readers will notice by the gap in pagination. Addressing the readers directly, Shandy explains in the following Chapter 25 that he is responsible for tearing out the chapter and proceeds to fill in some of the plot details:

> No doubt, Sir,—there is a whole chapter wanting here—and a chasm of ten pages made in the book by it—but the book-binder is neither a fool, or a knave, or a puppy—nor is the book a jot more imperfect (at least upon that score)—but, on the contrary, the book is more perfect and complete by wanting the chapter, than having it, as I shall demonstrate to your reverences in this manner...But before I begin my demonstration, let me only tell you, that the chapter which I have torn out, and which otherwise you would all have been reading just now, instead of this—was the description of my father's, my uncle Toby's, Trim's, and Obadiah's setting out and journeying to the visitation at.... (Sterne 1996 [1759]: 220)

As Walsh (1998: 90) explains, 'if chapter 24 were present, chapter 25 would not and could not exist' and that by filling in one gap 'inevitably leads to another somewhere else' (pp. 90–91). Sterne appears to distract readers by placing a greater importance on the construction of the book as the restored 10-page chapter is reduced to just a paragraph, thus inviting readers to imagine the missing events. These are the kinds of gaps that Iser (1978: 169) claims are central to his theory of reader response:

> Whenever the reader bridges the gaps, the communication begins. The gaps function as a kind of pivot on which the whole text-reader relationship revolves. Hence the structured blanks of the text stimulate the process of ideation to be performed by the reader on terms set by the text.

Textual gaps appear to be as much a part of the narrative where the emphasis appears to be on what did not take place or if they did are intentionally left out for effect, alongside those events that are explicitly told.

Possible Worlds Theory, Counterfactuality and Forked Paths

The previous sections in this chapter introduced the concepts of the *non-narrated*, *narrative refusals*, negation and textual gaps to explain the different ways that disnarration can be constructed. Disnarrated elements of the text foreground aspects of the narrative and invites readers to notice what is not there and fill in absences. Alternative scenarios generated by absences, hypothetical situations and divergences in the plotting of the story to offer counterfactual and possible worlds also invite attention. This section will outline Possible Worlds Theory as a philosophical concept to contextualise the existence of parallel universes with the concepts of counterfactual divergence and forked paths as further dimensions of narrative storytelling.

The notion of possible worlds was first proposed by the philosopher Gottfried Leibniz (1952 [1710]) in his work on semantics and truth conditions. Leibniz claimed that the world we inhabit is one of many possible worlds: this world is the *actual (or real) world* determined by where each individual is situated and by the Christian God, which exist as thoughts in the mind of God. Lewis (1978, 1986) explains possible worlds in terms of the concept of the plurality of worlds where all worlds—actual and possible worlds—are equal and equally existent but that an individual's existence is measured against a modal system that makes a distinction between the different worlds, known as *modal realism*. Actual and possible worlds exist independently of each other but only one world can be imagined because it is realised from the point of view of those who occupy them. In other words, the actual world depends on the position of the individual and their deictic centre so that ontologically, while all possible worlds exist, only one world can be actual among 'worlds which might have been or which could be' (Bell 2010: 20).

Many theorists have considered the application of possible worlds theory to fiction and storyworlds to understand the plurality and hierarchical worlds that exist within the narrative (see Bell 2010; Dannenberg 2008; Doležel 1998; Ryan 1991, 2013). Reading fictional texts requires a 'recentering' (Ryan 1991) so the shift from the actual world to the possible (fictional) world allows for a change to the frame of reference and all the possibilities within it. Ryan (1991: 3) uses the metaphor "world" to describe 'the semantic domain projected by the fictional text' as an ontological metaphor for fiction. The scenarios projected by possible worlds are systems of worlds or universes where one world functions as the actual domain, and many other worlds count as alternative possible states of the actual domain (Semino 2005; Ryan 1991). Characters who inhabit possible worlds constructed in the fictional storyworld will consider their world to be actual and real, so, exist in a 'textual actual world' (Bell 2016: 17) in the same way readers consider theirs as real because it is the only one that exists. The fictional universe is, for its characters, the actual world in this shift of possible worlds and even characters can experience possible worlds, for example in 'the privately imagined alternative worlds in their minds (wish-worlds, obligation-worlds and knowledge world)' (Fludernik 2009: 107). As Bell (2010: 20) explains:

> The actual world is surrounded by an infinite number of alternative states of affairs, which are known as possible worlds and they are generated by mental processes such as hopes, fears, wishes, dreams, hypothetical propositions and so on.

This statement is true of whoever is inhabiting and imagining the actual world at the point of the telling. Ryan (2013: 734) suggests that the audience's construction of narrative meaning involves establishing 'what holds as fact in the actual domain of the narrative universe, distinguishing the factual and physical from the possible and virtual located in the mental representations of characters. Furthermore, a narrative that is able to conjure up multiple non-actual possible worlds, for example, plots that involve deception rather than collaboration are seen as more interesting and a factor ensuring tellability because 'the reader is led to contemplate a richer semantic universe'. This also explains a reader's ability to make sense of complex world switches or plots beyond the realism of the actual world, such as the possible worlds created in science fiction, fantasy and surrealist texts.

Conceptualising fictional worlds from a specific deictic centre can also be explained by the literary and non-literary model of discourse processing called Text World Theory (Werth 1999; Gavins 2007). Text World Theory offers a cognitive-linguistic framework for the interpretation of fictional worlds—'a deictic space, defined initially by the discourse itself, and specifically by the deictic and referential elements in it' (Werth 1999: 180). Text World Theory is grounded in the metaphor TEXT AS A WORLD, and distinguishes between the real world of the readers called the discourse-world and the fictional world of the text called the text-world. Text World Theory allows readers to map their (schematic) knowledge and experience of the discourse-world to the spaces inhabited by characters in the text-world. This enables readers to understand the different levels of the story such as plot, characterization, narrators and authors and accept scenarios that differ significantly from the discourse-world. Gavins and Lahey (2016) explain that differences between Text World Theory and Possible Worlds Theory is that Text World Theory focuses on language as 'an interactive and negotiated event' (p. 2) so that the discourse-world is socially and culturally situated. Conversely, Possible Worlds Theory 'tends to be limited to an analysis of the ontological structures such language produces' and 'is as much grounded in the experiential principles of cognitive linguistics and cognitive psychology as it is in the ontology of possible-worlds semantics' (pp. 2–3). Text-worlds can be constructed linguistically through the conditional *if-clause* structure that generates alternative scenarios as it 'establishes an epistemic modal-world which has its status as an unrealized possibility made linguistically evident' (Gavins 2007: 120). In Text World Theory terminology, a shift into a further level of text-world called a sub-world is signalled by a range of semantic cues or world-building elements that include modal verbs as well as *if*-constructions. Werth (1999) divides the attitudinal sub-worlds communicating attitudes into three central areas of conceptual activity: 'desire' (or 'want-worlds') to express *wish, want, hope* and *dream*, 'belief' (or 'believe-worlds') based on truth assessments and 'purpose' (or 'intend-worlds') to convey the concept of intending future action and includes promises. For example, the character Charles in *The French Lieutenant's Woman* who, by imagining his future with Sarah, triggers the *desire* world-building element to create that sub-world.

Possible worlds inhabited by characters in a plot that takes place in a separate ontological space from the characters in their fictional/ story/text-world can also be conceptualised through the dimension of counterfactual storytelling. In *Coincidence and Counterfactuality*, Dannenberg (2008) draws on previous theoretical descriptions including those based on human counterfactualizing and psychology to offer a theory of counterfactuals in narrative fiction. She defines a counterfactual as 'a hypothetical alteration in a past sequence of events that changes the events in a *factual* sequence in order to create a different, *counter*factual outcome' (p. 119). The period before the alteration takes place is the ***antecedent*** and the period that follows as a result of the alteration is the ***consequent*** or ***outcome*** with ***upward*** and ***downward*** counterfactuals expressing positive (satisfaction) or negative (regret) experiences. Dannenberg (2008) also explains the distinction in the counterfactualizing agent where self-focused counterfactuals 'are made by a character who responds subjectively, and often emotionally to events in his or her life' (p. 119) versus externally-focused counterfactuals that analyse events, life stories, or history outside the speaker's own life. In other words, the self is either presented as a perpetrator (self-focus) or as a victim (external) of circumstances. The dimension of the disnarrated 'frequently consists of hopes, desires, imaginings and pondering, unreasonable expectations and incorrect beliefs' and also counterfactuals that are articulated as hypothetical modes. Dannenberg (2008: 116) clarifies the status of the counterfactual as disnarration stating it does not include counterfactual states 'articulated in the genre of alternate history, since here counterfactual events are narrated as actual events within the ontological hierarchy of the narrative world' and gives the example of Phillip K. Dick's (1962) *Man in the High Castle* where the Axis powers of Germany, Italy and Japan have won World War II.

Historical counterfactuals that are '***consciously virtual*** alternate versions of the past world' (Dannenberg 2008) ask ***what would have happened if?*** and propose a hypothetical deviation from real-world history and the conditions that would make this alternative version of the world exist. In a discussion of narrating the past as historical fiction, Robinson (2011: x) comments on the 'anachronistic narrative world' where present inquiry and past experience combine as events in the past are formulated through the present perspective. Robinson refers to this process as the present past where the emplotment of events can be described as 'partially counterfactual' as the historical fiction genre manages to merge fictional figures and events into scenarios that might be undocumented and not a true historical record. In these scenarios, there is a certain amount of improvisation which may go as far as blurring the lines between the real/discourse-world and the story/text-world. The main difference between history and historical fiction is that it is not possible to rewrite historical fact as it is fixed whereas a revisionist narrative is counterfactual, such as hypothesizing what might have happened if X had not won the election or a plot that ends with *Reader, I did not marry him*. As with more general works of fiction, historical fiction can also accommodate and present changes and forked paths through narration and characterization as the ending is not yet determined and therefore, open to alternative options. Roese and Olson (1995a, b) who take a social psychological approach to understanding the functions and motivations for counterfactual thinking, claim that creating alternative versions of past or present outcomes are part of human consciousness and that the negative effects of counterfactual thinking, such as unhealthy emotions, poor judgments, and counterproductive behaviour, can be influenced by individual character traits.

Counterfactual storytelling in fiction is a popular device for telling a good story. One well-known film whose plot hinges on the theme of counterfactual divergence is *Sliding Doors* (1998, directed by Peter Howitt). The film also gave rise to the expression 'sliding doors moment' to describe a single moment that can generate two alternative scenarios. *Sliding Doors* focuses on the protagonist, Helen whose life splits into two parallel universes as a result of a two-second delay when catching the train. Each parallel storyline contains the same characters and relationships, but each—as a result of a two second delay—follows a different plot based on luck and misfortune. At the point of counterfactual divergence where Helen's life forks, we see two Helens—one inside the train and one outside as the doors close, showing audiences the two counterfactual outcomes generated in one scene. Thereafter, we see Helen follow two separate paths as her narrative unfolds: having caught the train Helen arrives home early to find her boyfriend in bed with his lover and confronts him. She leaves her boyfriend, changes jobs to pursue her dreams and starts a new relationship (*path 1*). In the scenario where Helen misses the train, she is also mugged and as a result has to go to hospital. Because of this delay, she arrives home later than usual. She is unaware of her boyfriend's cheating and oblivious to his lies. She stays with him and experiences a less than satisfying (i.e. empowering) life (*path 2*).

Another example of counterfactual storytelling as a powerful plot device is found in Ian McEwan's (2001) metanarrative *Atonement* which was also made into a very successful film in 2007. Readers are told the story of Cecilia and Robbie as young lovers and their relationship that endured through the Second World War. It is not until the end that readers are made aware that the story is in fact a fictionalised account of their lives focalised through Briony, Cecilia's younger sister, who as an adult, narrates their story by looking back on past events. Readers are taken through the experiences of these characters from childhood to adulthood, sometimes intersecting and other times following their own paths (Robbie as a soldier, Cecilia as a nurse). The revelation at the end of the novel is therefore shocking as readers (and audiences of the 2007 film adaptation) are told that what they have experienced is an imagined, externally-focused counterfactual version of Cecilia and Robbie's lives. The now elderly Briony reveals that Cecilia and Robbie both died during the war (Robbie from sepsis, Cecilia in an underground tube shelter that was bombed) and the re-imagined version is Briony's attempt to atone for her terrible mistake decades earlier which resulted in separating Cecilia and Robbie and destroying their lives. Briony has spent the last 59 years redrafting a narrative where both Cecilia and Robbie were together. The actual events in the storyworld are disnarrated because they never happened and audiences are left to adjust their understanding of the story by shifting from Briony's counterfactual sub-world to the actual text-world of Cecilia and Robbie's tragic lives.

In Julian Barnes' (2011: 261) *The Sense of an Ending*, the character Tony Webster is also prone to counterfactual thinking when attempting to rationalise the consequences of his past actions:

> If… you had told me that Adrian, instead of killing himself, had counterfactually married Veronica, that they had had a child together…I would have answered: That's fine, each to their own life.

Tony tries to make sense of events that cannot be changed as he re-evaluates his life and expresses regrets for the serious consequences of his mistakes. Past actions and their consequences cannot be altered although counterfactual thinking allows us to glimpse alternative outcomes. Stories that provide virtual counterfactual plots where readers can imagine alternative scenarios for its characters include Chopin's *The Awakening* (1993 [1899]). The central character, Edna Pontellier chooses to commit suicide because she is unable to break free from the restrictions of her conventional life to one that would give her more freedom. Over time, readers see her hopes, desires and goals remain unfulfilled and this non-attainment generates possible *what if*? conditional statements about her unhappy state and her actions:

> If Edna had not acted on her initial impulses, she might have lived a long, unhappy life; or again, If Edna had not had an affair with Alcée Arobin, she might have drifted back into her passionless, stifling marriage with Léonce. (Herman 2002: 57. Italics in the original source)

Sadly, the hypothetical scenarios that express acts leading to positive outcomes remain conditional because they are never realised through the character's actions, or the narrator's or author's metadiegetic intrusion to manipulate the plot and allow Edna a happy ending.

Counterfactual divergences that generate alternative plots, paths and trajectories can also be described in terms of the forked path where the virtualities of a narrative are presented through the coexistence of contradictory pathways (Baroni 2016). The concept of plots that branch underlines Bremond and Cancalon's (1980) claim in *The Logic of Narrative Possibilities* that characters may create an alternative pathway for themselves whenever there is a decision to make and by doing so, influence and change the direction of the plot. This proposition is a direct response to Propp's (1968 [1928]) linear and goal-orientated plot structure that follows a single plot trajectory, which differs significantly from Bremond and Cancalon's (1980: 387) plot visualised as a 'network of possibilities' that characters may or may not experience. They explain that 'when the function which opens the sequence is proposed, the narrator always has the choice of having it followed by the act or of maintaining it in a state of virtuality'. The actualization of the act can either take place leading to the attainment of the goal, or not take place so the goal is not attained, that is, the act fails so the event 'can follow or not follow its course up to the end which was forseen'. The result is the opening up of a network of possibilities as illustrated in Fig. 2.1.

Bremond and Cancalon's concept of a network of plot possibilities explains how disnarration occurs so readily as it makes explicit the proposition that:

> every narrative function opens an alternative, a set of possible directions, and every narrative progresses by following certain directions as opposed to others: the disnarrated or choices not made, the roads not taken, possibilities not actualized, goals not reached. (Prince 1992: 36)

The roads not taken can be compared to the sub-worlds not generated, and the counterfactual alternatives only hypothesised alongside

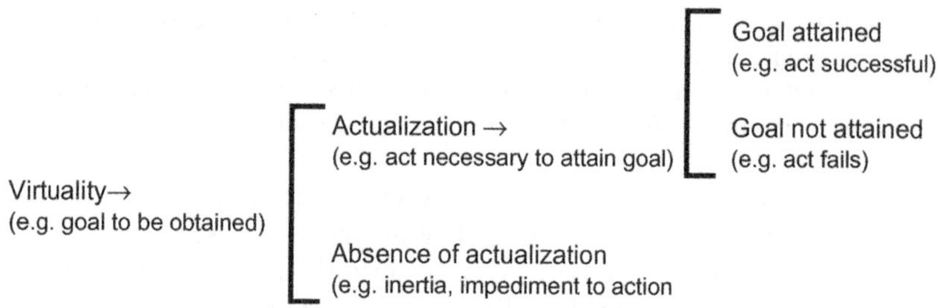

Fig. 2.1 Bremond and Cancalon's (1980) network of plot possibilities

the real path, and imagined through negation before being disnarrated. Bremond and Cancalon discuss their network of possibilities as a consequence of the decisions made by the narrator but it can also feel as though the characters also make choices. The contemporary novel *The Versions of Us* by Laura Barnett narrated by a heterodiegetic narrator hinges on a single event of a bike accident that is the catalyst that leads to Eva and Jim meeting before their story diverges into three separate paths with different outcomes. Whatever the trigger, it still falls to the characters and the choices they make to decide on the outcome of their initial meeting as in all three scenarios, Jim asks Eva for a drink and she has the choice to say 'yes' or 'no' to determine the various plot outcomes. *The French Lieutenant's Woman* (discussed in Chapter 5) makes the mechanics of fictional writing visible through narratorial intrusion where readers are told that characters can act wilfully and are beyond the control of the narrator. Characters and not the narrator are responsible for the plot options that develop and the mistakes that result from their actions.

Counterfactual divergence can easily be conceptualised in terms of the metaphorical forked path emerging at every point a plot option is taken, and also as a "labyrinth" that offers multiple possibilities. The notion of a forked path offering plot options derives from a short story by Jorge Luis Borges (2000 [1944]) called *The Garden of Forking Paths.* The story solves the mystery about the bifurcation or splitting of time when describing the chaotic and senseless manuscripts written by one Ts'ui Pên that 'constructs a labyrinth' (p. 50). Although the characters (one Stephen Albert and the I-narrator Yu Tsun, an ancestor of Ts'ui Pên) refer to a secret labyrinth in these manuscripts, they come to realise that the labyrinth is not a physical object but instead describes the novel itself which constructs a labyrinth. In other words, the forking is revealed to be in time and not in space and explains the curious '*I leave to the various futures (not to all) my garden of forking paths*' (p. 50). The story explains that each time a character makes a decision, a forked path is created at the point a choice is made. The scenario generates parallel pathways that exist simultaneously as opposed to one path being true and the other counterfactual, so that 'all possible outcomes occur: each one is the departure for other forkings' (p. 50). Yu Tsun explains:

> In all fictions, each time a man meets diverse alternatives, he chooses one and eliminates the others; in the work of the virtually impossible to disentangle Ts'ui Pên, the character chooses – simultaneously – all of them. He creates, thereby, 'several futures,' several times, which themselves proliferate and fork. (Borges 2000 [1944]: 51)

The result is a proliferation of multiple possibilities with each one creating multiple divergences as the story progresses. Baroni (2017: 248) points out that forked paths are central to hypertext fiction which rely on giving audiences multiple scenarios:

> Ts'ui Pên's book has often been associated with interactive storytelling, especially hypertext fictions and digital media. Indeed, in these kinds of narratives, all alternatives have been programmed or written and fully belong to the structure of the work itself, even though the reader (or the player) actualizes only one path, leaving the other paths unexplored.

In texts with numerous plot options, readers actively engage in plot progression by choosing available options to construct multiple counterfactual alternatives in the story (see Bell 2010). Generating counterfactuals achieve what Birke et al. (2001: 30) describe as a *contrast effect* because they 'sharpen the awareness of an actual state or outcome through the mental juxtaposition with a possible one'. The presence of disnarration, possible worlds and counterfactuality as narrative dimensions provide additional levels of narrativity in fictional stories: they challenge readers by offering hypothetical scenarios and choices where diversions, digressions and possibilities in the plot sequence and character actions play with expectations and invite new interpretations of the plot.

The Disnarrated and Counterfactual as Unnatural Narrative

Narratives that conjure up hypothetical, counterfactual and disnarrated scenarios defy many of the expectations of plot structure, temporality, narration and characterization because they offer approaches that depart from the familiar discourse-world. Readers readily expect improbable scenarios in fictional narratives across a range of genres, such as fairy tales with anthropomorphised animals or in science fiction with imaginative possible worlds and alien characters, but narratives situated in the discourse-world that suddenly split in time and space (e.g. *Sliding Doors*) are striking because they are inconceivable. Alber et al. (2010: 114) discuss the paradox of impossibilities in a mimetic storyworld with unconventional narrative strategies and explain:

> Most definitions of the term "narrative" have a clear mimetic bias and take ordinary realistic texts or "natural" narratives as being prototypical manifestations of narrative. That is to say, they focus far too extensively on the idea that narratives are modelled on the actual world and consequently ignore the many interesting elements of narrative which James Phelan has termed synthetic.

'Synthetic' elements provide innovative and challenging approaches to storytelling just as unconventional narrative dimensions offered by disnarration and *narrative refusals*, counterfactual divergence and impossible parallel plotlines do in the way they depart from realist texts. These types of narratives can be categorised as *unnatural narratives*, a subset of narrative fiction which describes texts that are anti-mimetic in their representation of real life. Alber (2013) explains:

> An unnatural narrative violates physical laws, logical principles, or standard anthropomorphic limitations of knowledge by representing storytelling scenarios, narrators, characters, temporalities, or spaces that could not exist in the actual world. However, narratives are never wholly unnatural; they typically contain 'natural' elements (based on real-world parameters) and unnatural components at the same time.

Unnatural narratives allow for a broad range of unconventional narrative techniques. They give storytellers 'free rein to the pleasures of the imagination, and they affirm the value of exploring what is not possible in extratextual reality' and in this way provide 'an alternative way of offering insight into that reality' (Phelan 2017: 51). Unconventional modes of narrative storytelling are likely to prompt readers to notice marked features of the text which simultaneously enhance the quality of its narrativity.

References

Abbott, H. P. (2008). *The Cambridge Introduction to Narrative* (2nd ed.). Cambridge: Cambridge University Press.

Abbott, H. P. (2013). *Real Mysteries, Narrative and the Unknowable*. Columbus, Ohio: Ohio State University.

Alber, J. (2013). Unnatural Narrative. In P. Hühn, J. C. Meister, J. Pier, & W. Schmid (Eds.), *The Living Handbook of Narratology*. Hamburg: Hamburg University. http://www.lhn.uni-hamburg.de/article/unnatural-narrative. Accessed 24 October 2018.

Alber. J., Iversen, S., Nielsen H. S., & Richardson, B. (2010). Unnatural Narratives, Unnatural Narratology: Beyond Mimetic Models. *Narrative, 18*(2), 113–136.

Austen, J. (1817). *Northanger Abbey*. London: John Murray.

Austen, J. (2003). *Northanger Abbey*. London: Penguin.

Barnes, J. (2011). *The Sense of an Ending*. New York: Alfred A. Knopf.

Barnett, L. (2015). *The Versions of Us*. London: Weidenfeld & Nicolson.

Baroni, R. (2016). Virtualities of Plot and Dynamics of Re-Reading. In R. Baroni & F. Revaz (Eds.), *Narrative Sequence in Contemporary Narratologies* (pp. 87–106). Columbus: Ohio State University Press.

Baroni, R. (2017). The Garden of Forking Paths: Virtualities and Challenges for Contemporary Narratology. In P. K. Hansen, J. Pier, P. Roussin, & W. Schmid (dir.), *Emerging Vectors of Narratology* (pp. 247–263). Berlin: de Gruyter, coll. Narratologia.

Bell, A. (1991). *The Language of News Media*. Oxford: Blackwell.

Bell, A. (2010). *The Possible Worlds of Hypertext Fiction*. Basingstoke: Palgrave-Macmillan.

Bell, A. (2016). "I Felt Like I'd Stepped Out of a Different Reality": Possible Worlds Theory, Metalepsis and Digital Fiction. In J. Gavins & E. Lahey (Eds.), *World Building: Discourse in the Mind* (pp. 15–32). London: Bloomsbury.

Birke, D., Butter, M., & Köppe, T. (2001). Introduction: England Win. In D. Birke, M. Butter, & T. Köppe (Eds.), *Counterfactual Thinking/ Counterfactual Writing* (p. 2). Berlin: Walter de Gruyter.

Borges, J. L. (2000 [1944]). The Garden of Forking Paths. In *Collected Fictions* (A. Hurley, Trans., pp. 119–128). London: Penguin.

Branigan, E. (1992). *Narrative Comprehension and Film*. London and New York: Routledge.

Bremond, C., & Cancalon, E. D. (1980). The Logic of Narrative Possibilities. *New Literary History, 11*(3), 387–411.
Bruner, J. (1991). The Narrative Construction of 'Reality'. *Critical Inquiry, 18*, 1–21.
Bruner, J. (1997). Labov and Waletzky Thirty Years On. *Journal of Narrative and Life History, 7*(1–4), 61–68.
Burke, K. (1945). *A Grammar of Motives*. New York: Prentice Hall.
Chatman, S. (1978). *Story and Discourse: Narrative Structure in Fiction and Film*. Ithaca, NY: Cornell University Press.
Chatman, S. (1990). *Coming to Terms: The Rhetoric of Narrative in Fiction and Film*. Ithaca: Cornell University Press.
Chopin, K. (1993 [1899]). *The Awakening* (N. A. Walker, Ed.). Boston: Bedford Books.
Cobley, P. (2014). *Narrative* (2nd ed.). London: Routledge.
Dancygier, B. (2012). *The Language of Stories: A Cognitive Approach*. Cambridge: Cambridge University Press.
Dannenberg, H. P. (2008). *Coincidence and Counterfactuality: Plotting Time and Space in Narrative Fiction*. Lincoln and London: University of Nebraska Press.
Dannenberg, H. P. (2014). Gerald Prince and the Fascination of What Doesn't Happen. *Narrative, 22*(3), 304–311.
Davis, W. A., Jr. (1997). The Rape of Tess: Hardy, English Law, and the Case for Sexual Assault. *Nineteenth-Century Literature, 52*(2), 221–231.
Dawson, P. (2018, April 18–22). *Creativity-Narrativity-Fictionality: A Critical Genealogy*. Paper presented to the International Conference on Narrative, McGill University, Montreal.
Dick, P. K. (2015 [1962]). *The Man in the High Castle*. London: Penguin.
Doležel, L. (1998). *Heterocosmica: Fiction and Possible Worlds*. Baltimore: Johns Hopkins University Press.
Fludernik, M. (1996). *Towards a 'Natural' Narratology*. London: Routledge.
Fludernik, M. (2009). *An Introduction to Narratology*. London: Routledge.
Forster, E. M. (1927). *Aspects of the Novel*. London: Edward Arnold.
Gavins, J. (2007). *Text World Theory: An Introduction*. Edinburgh: Edinburgh University Press.
Gavins, J., & Lahey, E. (2016). *World Building: Discourse in the Mind*. London: Bloomsbury.
Giovanelli, M. (2013). *Text World Theory and Keats' Poetry: The Cognitive Poetics of Desire, Dreams and Nightmares*. London: Bloomsbury.
Green, H. (1929). *Living*. London: Harvill Harper Collins.
Grice, H. P. (1975). Logic and Conversation. In P. Cole & J. Morgan (Eds.), *Syntax and Semantics* (Vol. 3, pp. 41–58). New York: Academic Press.

Hardy, T. (1891). *Tess of the d'Urbervilles*. London: James R. Osgood, McIlvaine & Co.
Hardy, D. (2003). *Narrating Knowledge in Flannery O'Connor's Fiction*. Columbia: University of South Carolina Press.
Hardy, D. (2005). Towards a Stylistic Typology of Narrative Gaps: Knowledge Gapping in Flannery O'Connor's Fiction. *Language and Literature, 14*(4), 363–375.
Herman, D. (2002). *Story Logic*. London: University of Nebraska Press.
Herman, D. (2003). Stories as a Tool for Thinking. In D. Herman (Ed.), *Narrative Theory and the Cognitive Sciences* (pp. 163–192). Stanford: CSLI Publications.
Herman, D. (Ed.). (2007). *The Cambridge Companion to Narrative*. Cambridge: Cambridge University Press.
Iser, W. (1978). *The Act of Reading*. London: Routledge.
Jeffries, L. (2010). *Critical Stylistics*. London: Palgrave Macmillan.
Joyce, J. (1914). *Dubliners*. London: Grant Richards Ltd.
Karttunen, L. (2008). A Sociostylistic Perspective on Negatives and the Disnarrated: Lahiri, Roy, Rushdie. *Partial Answers: Journal of Literature and the History of Ideas, 6*(2), 419–441.
Labov, W. (1972). *Language in the Inner City*. Philadelphia: University of Pennsylvania Press.
Labov, W. (1997). Further Steps in Narrative Analysis. *Journal of Narrative and Life History, 7*(1–4), 395–415.
Labov, W., & Waletzky, J. (1967). Narrative Analysis: Oral Versions of Personal Experience. In J. Holm (Ed.), *Essays on the Verbal and Visual Arts* (pp. 12–44). Seattle: University of Washington Press.
Leech, G. (1983). *The Principles of Pragmatics*. Harlow: Longman.
Leibniz, G. W. (1952 [1710]). *Theodicy* (E. M. Huggard, Trans.). London: Routledge.
Lewis, D. (1978). Truth in Fiction. *American Philosophical Quarterly, 1*, 37–46.
Lewis, D. (1986). *On the Plurality of Worlds*. Oxford: Blackwell.
Mandler, J., Scribner, S., Cole, M., & DeForrest, M. (1980). Cross-Cultural Invariance in Story Recall. *Child Development, 51*, 19–26.
McEwan, I. (2001). *Atonement*. London: Jonathan Cape.
Meyer, S. (2006). *Twilight*. London: Atom.
Michotte, M. (1963 [1946]). *The Perception of Causality* (T. R. Miles & E. Miles, Trans.). London: Methuen.
Miller, P. (1995). Personal Storytelling in Everyday Life: Social and Cultural Perspectives. In R. S. Wyer (Ed.), *Knowledge and Memory: The Real Story: Advances in Social Cognition* (Vol. 8, pp. 177–184). London, UK: Lawrence Erlbaum Associates.

Miller, P., & Moore, B. B. (1989). Narrative Conjunctions of Caregiver and Child: A Comparative Perspective on Socialization Through Stories. *Ethos: Journal of the Society for Psychological Anthropology, 17*(4), 428–449.

Miller, P. J., Fung, J., & Mintz, J. (1996). Self-Construction Through Narrative Practices: A Chinese and American Comparison of Early Socialization. *Ethos, 24*(2), 237–280.

Montoro, R. (2018). The Creative Use of Absences, a Corpus Stylistic Approach to Henry Green's Living. *International Journal of Corpus Linguistics, 23*(3), 279–310.

Mosher, H. F., Jr. (1993). The Narrated and Its Negatives: The Nonnarrated and the Disnarrated in Joyce's *Dubliners. Style, 27,* 407–427.

Mukařovsky, J. (1964 [1932]). Standard Language and Poetic Language. In P. Garvin (Ed.), *A Prague School Reader on Aesthetics, Literary Structure and Style* (pp. 17–30). Washington, DC: Georgetown University Press.

Ochs, E., & Capps, L. (2001). *Living Narrative.* Cambridge, MA: Harvard University Press.

Phelan, J. (2017). *Somebody Telling Somebody Else, a Rhetorical Poetics of Narrative.* Columbus: Ohio State Press.

Popova, Y. (2015a). Narrativity. In V. Sotirova (Ed.), *The Bloomsbury Companion to Stylistic* (pp. 488–506). London: Routledge.

Popova, Y. (2015b). *Stories, Meaning and Experience: Narrativity and Enaction.* London: Routledge.

Prince, G. (1982). *Narratology: The Form and Functioning of Narrative.* Berlin: Mouton.

Prince, G. (1988). The 'Disnarrated'. *Style, 22*(1), 1–8.

Prince, G. (1992). *Narratives as Theme: Studies in French Fiction.* London: University of Nebraska Press.

Prince, G. (2003). *Dictionary of Narratology.* Lincoln and London: University of Nebraska Press.

Prince, G. (2005). Narrativity. In D. Herman, M. Jahn, & M.-L. Ryan (Eds.), *Routledge Encyclopedia of Narrative Theory* (pp. 387–388). London: Routledge.

Propp, V. (1968 [1928]). *Morphology of the Folktale.* Austin: University of Texas Press.

Ricouer, P. (1980). Narrative Time. In W. J. T. Mitchell (Ed.), *On Narrative* (pp. 165–186). Chicago: Chicago University Press.

Robinson, A. (2011). *Narrating the Past: Histography, Memory and the Contemporary Novel.* Hampshire: Palgrave Macmillan.

Roese, N. J., & Olson, J. M. (Eds.). (1995a). *What Might Have Been: The Social Psychology of Counterfactual Thinking.* Mahwah, NJ: Lawrence Erlbaum Associates.

Roese, N. J., & Olson, J. M. (Eds.). (1995b). Counterfactual Thinking: A Critical Overview. In *What Might Have Been: The Social Psychology of Counterfactual Thinking*. Hillsdale, NJ: Lawrence Erlbaum Associates.

Rosaler, R. (2016). *Conspicuous Silences*. Oxford: Oxford University Press.

Ryan, M.-L. (1991). *Possible Worlds, Artificial Intelligence, and Narrative Theory*. Bloomington: Indiana University Press.

Ryan, M.-L. (2005). 'Tellability'. In D. Herman, M. Jahn, & M.-L. Ryan (Eds.), *Routledge Encyclopedia of Narrative Theory* (pp. 589–591). London: Routledge.

Ryan, M.-L. (2007). Toward a Definition of Narrative. In D. Herman (Ed.), *The Cambridge Companion to Narrative* (Cambridge Companions to Literature, pp. 22–36). Cambridge: Cambridge University Press.

Ryan, M.-L. (2013). Possible Worlds. In P. Hühn, J. C. Meister, J. Pier, & W. Schmid (Eds.), *The Living Handbook of Narratology*. Hamburg: Hamburg University. http://www.lhn.uni-hamburg.de/article/possible-worlds. Accessed 8 October 2017.

Sacks, H. (1992). *Lectures on Conversation*. Oxford: Blackwell.

Schank, R. C., & Abelson, R. P. (1995). Knowledge and Memory: The Real Story. In R. S. Wyer, Jr. (Ed.), *Knowledge and Memory: The Real Story* (pp. 220–231). Hillsdale, NJ: Lawrence Erlbaum Associates.

Scholes, R., & Kellogg, R. (1966). *The Nature of Narrative*. New York: Oxford University Press.

Semino, E. (2005). Possible Worlds: Stylistics Applications. In K. Brown (Ed.), *Elsevier Encyclopaedia of Language and Linguistics* (pp. 777–782). London: Elsevier.

Shklovsky, V. (1991 [1925]). *Theory of Prose* (V. Benjamin Sher, Trans.). Normal: Illinois State University; Champaign, IL: Dalkey Archive Press.

Simpson, P., & Canning, P. (2014). Action and Event. In P. Stockwell & S. Whitely (Eds.), *The Cambridge Handbook of Stylistics* (pp. 281–299). Cambridge: Cambridge University Press.

Sliding Doors. (1998). Directed by Peter Howitt.

Spolsky, E. (2005). Gapping. In D. Herman, M. Jahn, & M.-L. Ryan (Eds.), *Routledge Encyclopedia of Narrative Theory* (pp. 193–194). London: Routledge.

Sternberg, M. (2010). Narrativity: From Objectivist to Functional Paradigm. *Poetics Today, 31*, 507–659.

Sterne, L. (1996 [1759]). *The Life and Opinions of Tristram Shandy, Gentleman*. York: R. & J. Dodsley.

Thackeray, W. M. (1848). *Vanity Fair*. London: Bradbury and Evans.

Todorov, T. (1977). *The Poetics of Prose*. Oxford: Blackwell.

Toolan, M. J. (2001). *Narrative, a Critical Linguistic Introduction* (2nd ed.). London: Routledge.

Walsh, T. (1998). *The Dark Matter of Words: Absence, Unknowing, and Emptiness in Literature*. Carbondale: University of Southern Illinois Press.

Warhol, R. R. (2005). Neonarrative; Or, How to Render the Unnarratable in Realist Fiction and Contemporary Film. In J. Phelan & P. Rabinowitz (Eds.), *A Companion to Narrative Theory* (pp. 220–231). Oxford: Blackwell.

Warhol, R. (2007). Narrative Refusals and Generic Transformation in Austen and James: What Doesn't Happen in Northanger Abbey and Spoils of Poynton. *Henry James Review, 28*(3), 259–268.

Warhol, R. (2010). "What Might Have Been Is Not What Is": Dickens's Narrative Refusals. *Dickens Studies Annual, 41*, 45–60.

Warhol, R. (2013). It Is of Little Use for Me to Tell You: George Eliot's Narrative Refusals. In A. Anderson & H. E. Shaw (Eds.), *Companion to George Eliot* (pp. 46–61). London: Wiley.

Waugh, P. (1984). *Metafiction: The Theory and Practice of Self-Conscious Fiction*. New York: Methuen.

Werth, P. (1999). *Text Worlds: Representing Conceptual Space in Discourse*. London: Longman.

Wilensky, R. (1983). Story Grammars Versus Story Points. *Behavioral and Brain Sciences, 6*, 579–623.

Wilson, P. (2000). *Mind the Gap, Ellipsis and Stylistic Variation in Spoken and Written English*. Harlow, Essex: Pearson Education Limited.

Wolff, T. (1996). Bullet in the Brain. In *The Night in Question* (pp. 200–206). Bloomsbury: London.

CHAPTER 3

Disnarration and the Unmentioned in Fact: Oral Narratives of Personal Experience

Abstract This Chapter examines the dimension of disnarration in the first of two case studies about experiential narratives and asks why people share stories of disnarrated experiences. The discussion centres on oral narratives of personal experience narrated by London-born Greek Cypriot children undertaken as part of an ethnographic study by the author. The study set out to understand narrative structure and lexico-grammatical variations that could be correlated to different factors, such as the narrator's social factors, story topic and storytelling setting (groups or one-to-one with the interviewer). The collected stories included a subset of personal experiences with disnarration to describe experiences that did not happen, articulated through negation and adverbs. Counterfactual '*what if*' scenarios were also narrated to describe *what might have happened* if the events had occurred. Disnarration in personal narratives is discussed for insights into why experiences where nothing happens are important for making sense of our lives and necessary for our socialisation.

Keywords Oral narratives · Personal experiences · Children's narratives · Disnarrated · Hypothetical scenarios · Negation · *Danger of death*

M. Lambrou, *Disnarration and the Unmentioned in Fact and Fiction*, https://doi.org/10.1057/978-1-137-50778-5_3

Background

This chapter explores the dimension of disnarration in the oral narratives of personal experiences narrated by children who are members of the Greek Cypriot community in London (see Lambrou 2005, 2007). The data presented in this chapter emerged from a wider ethnographic study undertaken in 2000–2002 by the author to investigate the notion of a universal narrative structure based on oral narratives of personal experience. The study set out to investigate types of lexico-grammatical variation and attempt to correlate marked findings to a range of factors such as the speaker's social factors (gender, age, ethnicity), the interview setting for insights into how the dynamics with other people might affect the process of narration (peer group or one-to-one settings) and the story topic to investigate whether certain topics (danger of death, embarrassing, fight/argument, funny, happy and sad personal experiences) created variation in story structure. The informants for the study were in three age groups (9–12, 18–21 and 35–49) to also gain insights on cognitive and social influences for how stories develop. This chapter describes the disnarrated narratives by the youngest informants aged 9–12. The motivation for the initial study was to replicate Labov and Waletzky's (1967) and Labov's (1972) ground-breaking research into the personal narratives of members of the Black and Hispanic communities that led to the development of their schematic model of a narrative to "test" the universal claims of their narrative model. The London Greek Cypriot community was specifically chosen as they represent an alternative speech community to the one investigated by Labov and Waletzky and therefore one way of testing the presumed universalism of narrative structure. (As a member of the Greek Cypriot community in London, I had access to informants, which also helped greatly.) The aim, therefore was to identify *where* and *why* variation in personal narratives might exist, while attempting to provide further insights into cultural models for narratives. The model of narrative proposed by Labov and Waletzky comprises six schemas or section in the following order, each with a specific function in the narrative telling: *abstract*, *orientation*, *complicating action*, evaluation, *resolution*, *coda*. (See Chapter 2, *Narrative Models* for a discussion of Labov and Waletzky's model and Table 2.1 for a description of the functions of each schema.)

The ethnographic study involved asking all informants the same questions to prompt personal experiences, in both the one-to-one interview settings and peer group settings (two or more informants of the same age and gender) to put in place similar variables in the interview schedule. It was important that the experience actually occurred and that the person telling the story did not make it up or narrate a vicarious experience. The range of questions to elicit personal experiences on specific themes were as follows:

- *Can you tell me about a time you thought your life was in danger?*
- *Can you tell me about an embarrassing experience?*
- *Can you tell me about a happy experience?*
- *Can you tell me about a sad experience?*
- *Can you tell me about a time you were involved in a fight or an argument that really upset you?*

A total of 44 informants participated in 26 separate interviews and a corpus of 279 personal experiences were collected (see Lambrou 2005, 2007). An example of a *danger of death experience* is given in Table 3.1, by children (males), aged 10–11 in a peer group interview. The narrative has been presented to show the various stages of Labov and Waletzky's (1967) schema categories in the right-hand column. (All informants are anonymised and represented by the first letter of their name. In all interviews I was the interview or Int.)

Structurally, the personal narrative in Table 3.1 is 'fully-formed' as it comprises all six sections of Labov and Waletzky's narrative schemas,

Table 3.1 *Danger of death* narrative; aged 10–11; males; peer group interview

L	... em it's a danger one	*abstract*
	[em I was riding my bike cause I was going down a hill and	*orientation*
	you can't really see it cause there's another corner cause	*orientation*
	me and my friends were riding bikes and we were -both	*orientation*
	came out at the same time	*orientation*
	and we just -I don't know	*evaluation*
	um I smashed my chin and had to go to hospital	CA
	and had seven stitches inside my mouth	*resolution*
	and it really hurt	*evaluation*
	so and I was like I didn't ride my bike for another 3 or 4	*coda*
	months so	*coda*
Int	did it hurt when you tried to eat or talk?	
L	yeah a bit and I -after five months I got used to it and yeah ...	*evaluation*

categorised according to the 'group of clauses of a common functional type' (Labov 1997: 403). The narrated experience addresses the question asked by the interviewer at the start of the peer group interview (not shown) and repeated by the child in line 1 to frame their response with a relevant experience and signal they are about to take the floor to begin their story. The interviewer's question functions as the *abstract* and explains why this element of the personal experience may not always appear at the start of the informants' personal experience. In peer group interviews, the storytelling activity was found to be highly collaborative with children self-selecting one after the other to tell their story without the need for prompting by the interviewer (see Lambrou 2003).

Analysis of children's personal narratives, as in example Table 3.1, mostly corresponded with Labov and Waletzky's findings and included experiences that were not always as fully-formed as those of more skilful (and practiced) older narrators. For example, experiences were not always evaluated. What stood out was that as well as narrating experiences of what actually happened with a *complicating action* that led to a high point to satisfy and fulfil the interview question, some of the children also narrated experiences about events that did not happen (which I described as *almost narratives* before a deeper understanding of disnarration. See Lambrou 2005, 2007). The *almost narratives* were striking because they followed the Labovian trajectory of a temporally ordered narrative with an *orientation* and the beginnings of a *complicating action* with some *evaluation*. However, the *complicating action* and the *resolution*, the final part of the sequence of events stating what finally happened, subverted the expected point of the reason for the telling. What emerged was an experience that in the final stages of the narration, did not happen. In other words, the narrated experience was disnarrated. Examples of disnarrated experiences are given in Tables 3.2, 3.3, 3.4, and 3.5 with the clauses conveying disnarration emphasised in bold.

Table 3.2 *Danger of death* narrative; aged 10–11; males; peer group interview

Int	that's a funny story anything else?	
G	Yeah I got like a danger one	*Abstract*
	cause once I was on my blades yeah and we went to this	*Orientation*
	park and me and my friends we were doing loads of tricks	*Orientation*
	and there was this really steep hill I went up it and when I	*Orientation*
	was coming down there was this little coke can and	*Orientation*
	I tripped over it	*CA*
	and I wasn't wearing any pads or anything	*Orientation*
	and I literally like nearly broke my knee and shattered it	***Disnarration***
	but I didn't	***Disnarration***
	and it was all cut cause it was like it was stone ground and	*Evaluation*
	there was loads of like pebbles and like glass on it and it was	*Evaluation*
	really badly injured	*Evaluation*
Int	Did you have to go to hospital?	
G	No	*Coda*

In Table 3.2, G's personal narrative follows the trajectory of Labov and Waletzky's narrative structure providing the listener with an *abstract* (*I got like a danger one*, line 2), a detailed *orientation* (ll.3–6) and the beginnings of *complicating action* 'I tripped over it' (l.7). Instead of elaborating on what happened after tripping to fulfil the criteria of tellability, the narrator adds the anticlimactic 'and I literally like nearly broke my knee and shattered it but I didn't' (ll.9–10). The child still injured himself (ll.11–13) but not to the extent presented by the imagined 'nearly' broken and 'shattered' knee. The less serious outcome of the accident is confirmed with the child not needing to go to the hospital (ll.14–15). Listeners expect that when a person self-selects to narrate a personal narrative about danger, a traumatic experience will follow. The use of the intensifier *literally* which builds up the events leading to the accident also promise this outcome. However, the experience is negated by the adverb *nearly* which confirms that however close it was to the accident happening, it did not. G's personal narrative fits Prince's (2003: 22) category of events that do not happen 'but, nonetheless, are referred to (in a negative or hypothetical mode) by the narrative text'. Disnarrated personal narratives then raise the question why these types of experiences are shared, especially in a peer group setting with other children where they are likely to be evaluated. The expectation is to tell the most tellable of experiences within the theme of *danger of death* and yet something else spontaneously emerges in this peer group storytelling setting.

Another example of personal narratives about events that do not happen is presented in Table 3.3, with children in a peer group interview setting also responding to requests for *danger of death* experiences.

Both V and C's personal narratives may be minimal in their description of events but nevertheless appear to follow a conventional narrative trajectory as each begins with an *orientation* section providing clauses to contextualise their experience (l.3 and ll.10–12). Each informant then provides the opening clauses for the *complicating action* (l.4 and l.13).

Table 3.3 *Danger of death* narrative; aged 10–11; males; peer group interview

Int	Okay…okay have any of you been em in a situation where	*Abstract*
	there was a lot of danger and you were very frightened…?	*Abstract*
V	I was quite little and I went to cross the road and	*Orientation*
	this car went skidded	*CA*
	and it almost hit me	***Disnarration***
	and I got really scared…	*Evaluation*
Int	Were you okay?	
V	Yeah	*Coda*
Int	What about you two?	
C	[ ] I-I remember once when I walked [ ] crossed the road	*Orientation*
	as well and this car just came [ ] cause I was -like I never	*Orientation*
	looked where I was going I just looked straight	*Orientation*
	and I crossed the road	*CA*
	and this car nearly hit me…	***Disnarration***
Int	Hmm… okay …	

Instead of narrating details leading to the central claim for the danger of death experience, primed by the mention of the danger from the oncoming cars, audiences are told the car 'almost hit me' (l.5) and 'nearly hit me' (l.14) thus expressing scenarios that did not happen. The unrealised (and terrible) events as a consequence of car accidents are only imagined by the narrators and interpreted by the listeners. Another experience of an unrealised event is narrated in the *danger of death experience* in Table 3.4. The consequence of touching the ice (possibly liquid nitrogen) prompts

Table 3.4 *Danger of death* narrative; aged 10; males; peer group interview

D	...I was in my dad's work in the lab and we were [clears	*Orientation*
	throat] he's got he's got this tub where it's really freezing	*Orientation*
	minus some –a lot and em he keeps bacteria something in	*Orientation*
	there to keep them preserved and I was looking at it it was	*Orientation*
	open and I was looking at it and I thought "oh look it's ice"	*Orientation*
	so I got –	*Orientation*
	I started putting my hand in it	*CA*
	cause if I put my hand in it it would just be chopped off	***Disnarration***
	then my dad said "NO DON'T!"	*CA*
	you know	*Evaluation*
	took my hand away em ...	***Disnarration*** */Resolution*

the narrator to speculate on a *what if*? conditional scenario where his hand *would just be chopped off* (l.8) had his dad not called out to in time.

In Table 3.5, M's personal experience prompts a personal narrative about her inflamed appendicitis. It begins with a detailed *orientation* providing the *who?*, *what?*, *when? and where?* context but is disnarrated before any danger occurs. The experience 'but then I didn't have it out because it it deflamed' (l.12) is negated with 'didn't' again subverting the expectation of the narrative theme for a tellable narrative. All the above examples of disnarrated personal experiences where 'X didn't happen'; 'Y could have happened but didn't' (Prince 2003: 22) are embedded as part of the *resolution* that finalises the *complicating action*. The experience ends with

Table 3.5 *Sad* (*danger of death*); aged 10–12; female; peer group interview

Int	Okay we covered all the all the topics I just wonder if you	*Abstract*
	know maybe you've thought of another one like a happy	
	sad funny embarrassing fight or upset	
M	=Well em it's kind of sad but its happy in a way as well	*Abstract*
	em when I was seven I in January I em I got appendicitis	*Orientation*
	and I went to the hospital to have my appendix out and	*Orientation*
	em it it	*Orientation*
	I was really scared cause I was only seven	*Evaluation*
	and my dad said if I have my appendix out I could go to	*Orientation*
	Venice em if I don't get it out I have to go to Bognor Regis	*Orientation*
	which sounded like really horrible em	*Evaluation*
	but then I didn't have it out because it it deflamed	***Disnarration***
	so em that was okay ...	*Evaluation/Coda*

nothing reportable happening with the narrative leading towards a presumed high point that describes events, that is, the thing which does not happen.

Taking the floor for an extended turn should be justified (Sacks et al. 1974) and in interactive peer group interviews where self-selection takes place (instead of the speaker being allocated) a narrative that fulfils the criteria of having narrativity would be expected. As Ricouer (1980: 174) explains, stories are expected to have an acceptable conclusion and while his discussion is based on fictional stories, this is also a requirement for experiential narratives:

> Following a story, [...] we are pushed ahead by this development and that we reply to its impetus with expectations concerning the outcome and the completion of the entire process. In this sense, the story's conclusion is the pole of attraction, of the entire development. But a narrative conclusion can be neither deduced nor predicted. There is no story if our attention is not moved along by a thousand contingencies. That is why a story has to be followed to its conclusion. So rather than being predictable, a conclusion must be acceptable.

Where a conclusion is not acceptable, the effect on audiences is likely to cause *schema disruption* as the 'conceptual deviance offers a potential challenge' (Stockwell 2002: 79). Existing knowledge structures are undermined and audiences may even question whether what they have heard is in fact a narrative.

Disnarrated Personal Narratives: Form and Function

A closer analysis of the linguistic form and function of disnarrated personal experiences to identify the ways disnarration is communicated is presented below with an explanation of why these types of experiences are nevertheless cognitively enabling. As with conventional narratives, disnarrated experiences also permit us to make sense of life events by encoding vital information of alternative states of affairs and that sharing them is necessary for our socialisation.

Form

The disnarrated experiences in Tables 3.1–3.5 describing what does not happen in personal experiences are communicated through a range of linguistic strategies categorised as ***adverbs***, ***negation*** and ***conditional*** clauses as set out in Table 3.6.

The use of degree adverbs, negation with the auxiliary did+not+verb, and the conditional *if*+would structure for a hypothetical scenario draws attention to the different ways experiences that do not happen can be narrated. The adverbs of degree ***almost*** and ***nearly*** modify the verb (hit, fell) to describe how close the danger was to actually happening and

Table 3.6 Linguistic forms of disnarration in children's personal narratives

Linguistic form	*Examples from personal narratives*
Adverbs (degree)	this car went skidded and it **almost** hit me this car **nearly** hit me I **nearly** fell off the cliff in a car I was **almost** hit by a rugby ball
Negation (auxiliary did+not)	I literally like nearly broke my knee and shattered it but I **didn't** I **didn't** have it out [the appendix]
Conditional *if+would clause*	**if** I put my hand in it it **would** just be chopped off

offers a rich approach to storytelling. Labov and Waletzky (1967) and Labov (1972: 366) also identified a range of lexical devices as part of the ***evaluation*** described as ***internal evaluation*** (the other being ***external evaluation***) where evaluative strategies are woven into the story to convey how the narrator felt. Labov and Waletzky organised the types of ***internal evaluation*** under four categories: ***intensifiers***, ***comparators***, ***correlatives*** and ***explicatives***. The most relevant to the discussion of disnarration in children's narratives are the comparators that describe negatives, conditionals and adverbs, as set out in Table 3.7.

Table 3.7 Types of comparators (internal evaluation) (From Lambrou 2005: 82)

Internal evaluation: Comparators
Evaluate indirectly by comparing events which occurred to those which did not; are sources of syntactic complexity, include:

- **negation**
- **modality and modulation** (modal verbs and adverbs)
- **futurity**
- **hypothetical sentences**
- **questions** (usually embedded in the speech of the narrators)
- **imperatives**
- **comparative or superlative phrases** (with *as* in prepositional phrases and *like* in metaphors and similes)

Unrealized events that are compared with realized ones, or comparators, function to express what could have happened or what Labov (1972) describes as irrealis clauses. According to Labov (1972: 381) comparators 'provide a way of evaluating events by placing them against a background of other events which might have happened, but did not' as they:

> draw upon a cognitive background considerably richer than the set of events which were observed. They provide a way of evaluating events by placing them against the background of other events which might have happened.

Labov found *comparators* to be more evident in personal narratives narrated by adults than those told by adolescents/pre-adolescents (compared to my data) suggesting they are associated with more complex and sophisticated storytellers. The use of negatives, or what Halliday and Matthiessen (2004) call 'negative polarity' to describe the choice between positive and negative constructions such as 'is' and 'isn't', is the marked feature because positive polarity tends to be the norm. Negative polarity can be compared to Leech's (1983) sub-maxim of 'negative uninformativeness' to account for negatives being more informative as they offer the opposite of the expected state of affairs. The effect of negation draws attention to what did not take place as much as what did so 'we need a particular reason for talking about what is not rather than what is' suggests Thompson (1996: 56). Unlike Labov's findings, disnarrated experiences only occurred in children's narratives and only in peer group interactions.

Function

Why are disnarrated experiences told when they undermine the important condition of reportability where 'a reportable event is one that justifies the automatic reassignment of speaker role to the narrator' (Labov 1997: 406). This section will attempt to understand why these types of narratives are told and why they are an important subgenre of storytelling in the personal experiences of children.

It has already been established that storytelling is a social activity and provides a medium to encode news, warnings and dilemmas, for example. As Culler (1997: 83) states, 'Stories [...] are the main way we make sense of things, whether in thinking of our lives as a progression leading somewhere or in telling ourselves what is "happening in the world"'. In the study involving children, all the examples of disnarrated experiences signalled with negation, conditional if+would structures and degree adverbs to convey events that did not happen are only in response to personal narratives about *danger of death* experiences where *Trouble* (with a large 'T') defines complication (Bruner 1991). Children are keenly aware of the various dangers they have avoided having reflected on and evaluated their experiences as demonstrated by articulating hypothetical consequences of what might have been. For children aged 10–12, disnarrated experiences represent the *most* dangerous experiences in their relatively young lives and small repertoire of danger experiences. They also appear to understand that these experiences encode moral and ethical values and that if shared, can warn others of possible serious and life-threatening danger. By visualising what could have happened had the events in the *complicating action* actually followed through to the *resolution*, the consequences presented by these alternative scenarios justify their telling. This is despite not seeming to fulfil the quality of tellability. The ellipses produced by the events of *what might have been* in the examples 'this car went skidded and it almost hit me' and 'this car nearly hit me' (in Table 3.5) and uses of negation especially, generate implicatures so audiences have to infer the outcomes. In *what+if* conditional scenarios, as in the example 'if I put my hand in it it would just be chopped off' (Table 3.4), hypothetical and counterfactual scenarios are triggered in the minds of listeners as the disnarrated consequence is explicitly referred to. These examples can also be described in terms of *evaluative stance* because they 'convey a particular point-of view toward the counterfactual scenario, and encourage the listener to understand and share the speaker's evaluation' (Riddle Harding 2007: 264). As an example of the seriousness with which audiences understand the imagined scenario, Riddle Harding (2007: 263) describes events that followed an attempted assassination in 1958 in New York City where Dr Martin Luther King was stabbed (emphasis in bold is mine):

> The *New York Times* reported the next day that **if he had sneezed, he would have died**. Later in a speech, King quoted a letter he received from a girl who wrote to him: I read in the paper of your misfortune, and of your suffering. And I read that **if you had sneezed, you would have died**. And I'm simply writing you to say that I'm so happy that you didn't sneeze.

As Riddle Harding points out, the girl clearly understood the consequences and added her own evaluation with 'I'm so happy that you did not sneeze' to express an attitude towards the counterfactual event and the preferred outcome.

Sharing *evaluation* is an important element in the interaction between storytellers and audiences. As I pointed out earlier in this section, all the disnarrated personal narratives narrated by children on the subject of *danger of death* scenarios occurred in peer group interviews only (with two or more children) and not in one-to-one interview settings (with one child and the interviewer). Peer group interviews allow children to participate by "performing" their experience and demonstrating *membership* of the group, even if nothing reportable happens. It can be argued that interactive contexts for storytelling encourages self-aggrandizement which is 'designed to place the narrator in the most favorable possible light' (Labov and Waletzky 1967: 34). Conversely, one-to-one interview settings are less likely to encourage this type of performance as there is no need to impress the interviewer where a more conventional question-answer interview dynamic ensues (which was certainly the case in my study.) Engaging in storytelling activities, especially among friends where there is likely to be an element of social pressure to construct a particular identity, also requires the narrator to demonstrate their skills as a narrator. In the wider study, Lambrou (2003, 2005) found children in peer group interviews to be highly competitive, often interrupting each other to take a turn and narrate their experiences so the interview shifted to what resembled a highly interactive group conversation as informants self-selected or selected each other to narrate their personal experiences.

This change 'unintentionally forces the interviewer into a role that is backgrounded' with less need for prompting. 'With talk becoming freer, the obvious advantage is that the interview becomes less inhibiting for the production of narrative story-telling' (Lambrou 2003: 155). This type of collaborative storytelling appears to be a marked feature of group storytelling contexts as children prompt and trigger often similar experiences in other children through *direct* and *indirect prompts* (see Lambrou 2003, 2005).

Features of competition and collaboration were also found in Meng's (1992) study of narrative storytelling development in young German children where it is important to participate as part of the group. Ochs and Capps (2001: 71) also discuss tellability in children's personal narratives, stating that 'the roots of highly tellable narratives may be located in children's awareness of unexpected events' and indicates their awareness of what is expected and normative. Events that are outside this category are narrated more to 'reflect upon temporal and causal ordering of canonical events in their life' as well as 'clarify basic routines of import [...] including variations in daily activities' (p. 78). Narrating personal experiences then are 'cognitively enabling' (Toolan 2001: 13) because they help individuals shape their lives and plan for the future.

The personal narratives in my study show the clear correlation between *danger of death* scenarios and disnarration so that *Trouble* (with a capital 'T') plays an important factor in prompting these stories where accidents, maiming and even death may be a consequence. Disnarrated experiences were not present in *happy* and *funny* experiences that produced positive experiences where nothing bad happens to the narrator or to anyone else. Interestingly, children's literature provides a model for storytelling with mostly positive outcomes which follow the requirement of being 'optimistic with happy endings [...] presented from the viewpoint of innocence' (Nodelman 1992: 190. See also, Pape 1992 on the literary convention of happy endings in children's literature). Traditionally fairy tales as well as more contemporary children's fiction such as the *Harry Potter* series, present children with existentialist dilemmas that are traumatic, such as the loss of a parent at the start of the story. Children are also presented with difficult obstacles to overcome and baddies to beat in order to reach the final, happy outcome. Children nowadays, however, are presented with a much broader range of narrative themes and plots from an early age, which is likely to affect their knowledge of story schemas. Other work on endings in fictional narratives discuss endings in terms of *closure* which 'has to do with a broad range of expectations and uncertainties that arise in the course of a narrative and that part of us [...] hopes to resolve or close' (Abbott 2008: 57. See also Abbott 2005). The concept of closure brings the narrative to a complete and satisfactory resolution. Kermode (1968) describes two different types of closure as *structural closure* pertaining to the plot and *psychological closure*, pertaining to the protagonist's personal conflicts, while Abbot (2005: 66) referring to Rabinowitz (1987) differentiates *inertial* from *non-inertial* endings, 'the one arriving according to expectations, the other not, yet neither necessarily yielding nor failing to yield closure'. In children's literature, *structural* and *psychological* endings are more likely to coincide to provide an expected and acceptable ending. Expectations that are not met are closer to Warhol's (2005, 2010, 2013) notion of the paranarratable, particularly if characters and plots are at odds with the storytelling genre and cultural expectations.

References

Abbott, H. P. (2005). Closure. In D. Herman, M. Jahn, & M.-L. Ryan (Eds.), *Routledge Encyclopedia of Narrative Theory* (pp. 65–66). London: Routledge.

Abbott, H. P. (2008). *The Cambridge Introduction to Narrative* (2nd ed.). Cambridge: Cambridge University Press.

Bruner, J. (1991). The Narrative Construction of 'Reality'. *Critical Inquiry, 18,* 1–21.

Culler, J. (1997). *Literary Theory.* Oxford: Oxford University Press.

Halliday, M. A. K., & Matthiessen, C. M. I. M. (2004). *An Introduction to Functional Grammar* (3rd ed.). London: Edward Arnold.

Kermode, F. (1968). *The Sense of an Ending.* Oxford: Oxford University Press.

Labov, W. (1972). *Language in the Inner City.* Philadelphia: University of Pennsylvania Press.

Labov, W. (1997). Further Steps in Narrative Analysis. *Journal of Narrative and Life History, 7*(1–4), 395–415.

Labov, W., & Waletzky, J. (1967). Narrative Analysis: Oral Versions of Personal Experience. In J. Holm (Ed.), *Essays on the Verbal and Visual Arts* (pp. 12–44). Seattle: University of Washington Press.

Lambrou, M. (2003). Collaborative Oral Narratives of General Experience: When an Interview Becomes a Conversation. *Language and Literature, 12*(2), 153–174.

Lambrou, M. (2005). *Story Patterns in Oral Narratives: A Variationist Critique of Labov and Waletzky's Model of Narrative Schemas* (Unpublished PhD thesis). Middlesex University, London.

Lambrou, M. (2007). Oral Accounts of Personal Experiences: When Is a Narrative a Recount? In M. Lambrou & P. Stockwell (Eds.), *Contemporary Stylistics* (pp. 195–208). London: Continuum.

Leech, G. (1983). *The Principles of Pragmatics*. Harlow: Longman.

Meng, K. (1992). Narrating and Listening in Kindergarten. *Journal of Narrative and Life History, 2*(3), 235–276.

Nodelman, P. (1992). *The Pleasure of Children's Literature*. London: Longman.

Ochs, E., & Capps, L. (2001). *Living Narrative*. Cambridge, MA: Harvard University Press.

Pape, W. (1992). Happy Endings in a World of Misery: A Literary Convention Between Social Constraints and Utopia in Children's and Adult Literature. *Poetics Today, 13*(1), 179–196.

Prince, G. (2003). *Dictionary of Narratology*. Lincoln and London: University of Nebraska Press.

Rabinowitz, P. (1987). *Before Reading: Narrative Conventions and the Politics of Interpretation*. Columbus: Ohio State Press.

Ricouer, P. (1980). Narrative Time. In W. J. T. Mitchell (Ed.), *On Narrative* (pp. 165–186). Chicago: Chicago University Press.

Riddle Harding, J. (2007). Evaluative Stance and Counterfactuals in Language and Literature. *Language and Literature, 16*(3), 263–280.

Sacks, H., Schegloff, E. A., & Jefferson, G. (1974). A Simplest Systematics for the Organization of Turn-Taking for Conversation. *Language, 50*(4), 696–735.

Stockwell, P. (2002). *Cognitive Poetics*. London: Routledge.

Thompson, G. (1996). *Introducing Functional Grammar*. London: Arnold.

Toolan, M. J. (2001). *Narrative: A Critical Linguistic Introduction* (2nd ed.). London: Routledge.

Warhol, R. R. (2005). Neonarrative; Or, How to Render the Unnarratable in Realist Fiction and Contemporary Film. In J. Phelan & P. Rabinowitz (Eds.), *A Companion to Narrative Theory* (pp. 220–231). Oxford: Blackwell.

Warhol, R. (2010). "What Might Have Been Is Not What Is": Dickens's Narrative Refusals. *Dickens Studies Annual, 41*, 45–60.

Warhol, R. (2013). It Is of Little Use for Me to Tell You: George Eliot's Narrative Refusals. In A. Anderson & H. E. Shaw (Eds.), *Companion to George Eliot* (pp. 46–61). London: Wiley.

CHAPTER 4

Disnarration and the Unmentioned in Fact: News Stories

Abstract This chapter presents the second discussion on disnarration in factual texts and examines the reporting of events that do not happen in news stories. The chapter begins by establishing the criteria for news values by drawing on Galtung and Ruge (1965) and Bell's (1991) influential list of news criteria to understand what makes news stories newsworthy as a context for disnarration. Examples of disnarrated events in news stories are discussed by applying Bednarek and Caple's (2014) discourse analytic framework of news values where the focus is on the range of linguistic devices that construct newsworthiness. Central to the reportability of disnarrated news stories is the audience's understanding of the terrible consequences had the averted outcomes in the news stories occurred, triggered through counterfactual thinking and the prominence of the news value of *NEGATIVITY*. It is this ability to speculate on the counterfactual that appears to justify why extraordinary events where nothing happens are nevertheless considered as newsworthy.

Keywords News values · News discourse · Newsworthiness · Near miss scenarios · Counterfactual thinking · Disnarration · Negation

M. Lambrou, *Disnarration and the Unmentioned in Fact and Fiction*,
https://doi.org/10.1057/978-1-137-50778-5_4

Introduction

In this second chapter on factual narratives, news stories are examined for the dimension of disnarration and the unmentioned to understand the relevance of these types of stories as newsworthy. As with personal narratives, which are expected to be tellable and fulfil criteria for their telling, news stories are also expected to fulfil specific news values to ensure that they are newsworthy and reportable. News discourse is about both what happened and the importance of 'what we are *told*' (Bell 1998: 65) and adhere to a specific register and event structure. However, events in the news that are disnarrated appear to contradict expectations of newsworthiness and this chapter attempts to explore why these events are reported and published widely and justify being an important part of the news agenda.

News Stories

News stories construct experiences that occur on a daily basis and in the wider society and similar to personal narratives, both genres of storytelling help us to make sense of the world we live in. The news in particular, 'is important both for what it reveals about a society and because it also itself contributes to the character of society' (Bell 1998: 64–65). In fact, Bell (1991) describes journalists as professional storytellers of our age and instead of the *once upon a time* opening, a news story begins with factual events, as in the example 'Fifteen people were injured today when a bus plunged…' (Bell 1991: 147). Lule (2001: 3) states that 'news comes to us as a story' because we understand our lives through story and that news stories look to 'archetypal figures and forms to offer exemplary models for human life' (p. 15). He describes the important stories of mankind as *myths* that are 'a sacred, social story that draws from archetypal figures to offer exemplary models of human life' (p. 17). Lule (2001) identifies seven enduring myths called *master myths* that journalists tell and retell that provide alternative perspectives on society, which are: *the victim, the scapegoat, the hero, the good mother, the trickster, the other world* and *the flood* (p. 25). In the construction of news, audiences will also expect news stories to be based on facts (or at least sourced truthfully) and for journalists to be trustworthy, impartial and objective in their reporting of events with attribution playing an important role. Harcup (2009) notes that *impartial* and *objective* are used interchangeably but their meanings differ as impartial reporting equates to being neutral while objective reporting is based on verifiable facts.

As with traditional oral and literary narratives, news stories also follow a conventionalised and formulaic structure, commonly called the *inverted triangle* where the most important information is summarised first at the top, leading down to the least important. Critics of this structure point out that it depends on who decides what is important and that can affect where the information is placed in the triangle structure. News stories, as Bell (1991: 154) points out, are not always reported in chronological order, moving back and forth in time and if the news story is ongoing, it may not be resolved and finish 'mid-air'. Bell proposes a model for the discourse structure of news texts set out in a tree diagram with branches leading to sub layers where the first layer comprises:

Attribution (source, place and time)
Abstract (headline, lead)
Story (episode 1; event n).

The body of the story 'consists of one or more episodes, which in turn consist of one or more events' (providing further layers to the tree diagram) while events 'must describe actors and action, usually expressing setting of time and place' (Bell 1998: 67, see also Bell 1991). Hard news, which report on the important stories dealing with business, politics and international news are also expected to fulfil the core rhetorical function of the journalistic five Ws and *H*: the *who?*, *what?*, *where?*, *when?*, *why? how?* in the opening paragraph. (Newsprint also comprises different forms of news reporting that are stylistically distinct in form and content, such as the opinion-editorials, life-style and sports reporting.) The five W's and H are comparable to Labov and Waletzky's (1967) *orientation* section as they answer questions that contextualise the story before the central facts of the news events are reported. (The *what?* will also convey actual news—the reportable sequence of events.) The news headline can be compared to the *abstract* as it also functions to prime audiences about what the news story will contain as concisely as the space allows. Headlines also contribute to the initial tellability of the story as they strategically convey information to engage readers by foregrounding the important, interesting, unusual, dramatic and unexpected—through keywords and phrases. Unlike the Labovian model, the reporting of news events is not necessarily presented in a chronological order so 'it is at odds with the linear narrative point. It moves backwards and forwards in time, picking out different actions on each cycle' (Bell 1991: 153). It is therefore left to the reader 'to reassemble events in their experienced order insofar as the reader feels the need to do this' (Toolan 2001: 207). In fact, psychological studies of news comprehension found a tendency for audiences to reconstruct the order of news events in a chronological sequence (see Lutz and Wodak 1987; Duszak 1991). I suggest that a similar process of construction or "repair" occurs in news events that are disnarrated through negation or ellipses as readers are required to interpret the story by filling in any gaps to make sense of the story. Disnarrated stories rely on audiences to speculate on *what might have been* to comprehend alternative scenarios if the events occurred and news editors are aware of this fact. Examples of disnarrated news stories are provided in the following sections but before discussing this dimension of news, a brief overview of news values—the criteria that create newsworthiness—is outlined first to provide a context for understanding why disnarrated news events are considered tellable.

News Values and Newsworthiness

One of the best ways to exemplify the condition of newsworthiness is to consider the famous maxim, 'When a dog bites a man that is not news, but when a man bites a dog that is news' (credited to various people involved in creating news stories). The difference in the two events is that the latter event is more likely to be reported because it is an unusual and exceptional occurrence compared to the first event which is not. Unusual and exceptional events are likely to be favoured over events that are deemed to be common and not out of the ordinary and for these reasons will be considered to be newsworthy. (Narratologists would say that the latter state of affairs has more narrativity compared to the first.) A former editor of the *Times* and *Sunday Times*, Harold Evans (1972) identifies several conditions for news stories which is that they should be:

i. about necessary information and unusual events
ii. based on observable facts
iii. an unbiased account

iv. free from the reporter's opinion and the more news values a story has, the more likely it will be reported.

Events that are reportable must adhere to a set of guidelines and those events that are important over and above others are presented as the leading story to make the headlines. One of the most influential list of news values was compiled by Johan Galtung and Mari Ruge (1965) and looked at international news stories to understand which factors they had in common to make them reportable. They identified 12 news values, the qualities that make a story not simply informative but eligible for coverage as material suited to news and feature genres. Galtung and Ruge (1965) categorised the 12 news values under three subheadings: *Impact*, *Audience Identification* and *Pragmatics of media coverage* to organise their criteria:

Impact

FREQUENCY
THRESHOLD
REFERENCE TO SOMETHING NEGATIVE
UNEXPECTEDNESS
UNAMBIGUITY

Audience identification

REFERENCE TO PERSONS
MEANINGFULNESS
REFERENCE TO ELITE NATIONS
REFERENCE TO ELITE PEOPLE

Pragmatics of media coverage

CONSONANCE
CONTINUITY
COMPOSITION

Galtung and Ruge (1965: 64–65) state that 'No claim is made for completeness in the list of factors or "deductions"', however, it offers the 'foundation study' of news values (Bell 1991: 155). Spencer-Thomas (2005) points out that Galtung and Ruge argue that journalists tend to select stories with a high news value, that is, a high score on one or more of the news factors, suggesting that the values are not equally weighted in importance. Another criticism is that the list is based only on international news stories rather than lesser events. It could be argued that a news story is a news story whether, local, national or international, as it will adhere to the same set of criteria.

Since Galtung and Ruge's first offered their list of news values, there have been various revisions including those by Bell (1991: 156–158) who also proposed 12 news values some of which remained the same. See Table 4.1.

Table 4.1 News values (adapted from Bell 1991)

News value	*Description*
NEGATIVITY	Bad or negative
RECENCY	Has only just happened
PROXIMITY	Took place geographically close to the reader or viewer
CONSONANCE	Fits readers' or viewer's preconceptions or stereotypes about how the world is
UNAMBIGUITY	Is relatively clear-cut and unambiguous
UNEXPECTEDNESS	Is rare, unexpected or unpredictable
SUPERLATIVENESS	Is outstanding or superlative in some respect
RELEVENCE	Can be presented as relevant to the audience's own lives or experience
PERSONALISATION	Can be pictured in personal terms
ELITENESS	Involves news actors who are socially prominent in some respect
ATTRIBUTION	Comes from news sources who carry some kind of socially validated authority
FACTICITY	Consists of or can be supported by facts and figures

In their 2001 article, *What is news? Galtung and Ruge revisited*, Harcup and O'Neill revised the list further to include *power elite*, *celebrity* and *entertainment* as news values, while Niblock (2005) suggests there are other important criteria that make news. Niblock refers to the criteria as *in-built* characteristics of an event or issue which are *intrinsic* or *extrinsic news* values. Specifically, *intrinsic* news values 'appeal to the consensus views and values of the culture readers inhabit' and *extrinsic* news values 'relate closely to journalists' experience of the process of selection' (pp. 76–79). Bednarek and Caple's (2014) more recent study of news values claim that newsworthiness can be constructed and emphasised through language that conveys *NEGATIVITY*, *TIMELINESS*,

PROXIMITY and *SUPERLATIVENESS* and developed a framework for their analysis (which is discussed later in this chapter). The use of photographs, film, narration and music on and across newsprint, online and broadcast news provides multimodal dimensions for enhancing news reporting to make them more reportable, especially if dramatic scenes can be captured through image and sound as part of the news story.

Disnarration in News Stories

To understand how disnarration works in news reporting, consider the following. News values are most notably present in the story's headline and opening sentence to claim facticity, as in the examples of the single sentence news stories a. and b. below (from Bell 1998: 69):

a. **Clashes kill eight**
   At least eight people have died in tribal fighting in the Bimbila region of northern Ghana—AFT.
b. **Icicle horror**
   A woman was fighting for life last night after a giant icicle fell 30 storeys from a New York skyscraper and speared her.

Both sentences are likely to be a summary from the opening paragraph of a longer story and includes the journalist's *who?*, *what?* and *where?* criteria. Sentence a. has the news agency attribution (AFT) whereas sentence b. does not. Time is conveyed in b. ('last night') fulfilling the *when?* criteria but not in a. although readers will accept that the story is likely to have taken place in the last 24 hours before its coverage. The use of the passive verb form in b. ('was fighting') also points to a grammar of news discourse and both stories are about death or the threat of death. As Bell (1998) points out, in b. every news value is referenced: with 'fighting for life', 'giant' icicle' 'fell 30 storeys', 'New York skyscraper', and 'speared' ensuring that 'the facticity of the stories is stressed through the detail of person, place and time' (p. 76). A news story's facticity not only confirms accurate facts about the events but assumes the events actually happened to conform to the presupposed expectations of truth. An examination of examples of disnarrated news stories with a discussion of the discourse of disnarration will attempt to understand why these events are of interest and provide an important subcategory of news story.

On the 13 October 2015, the BBC online website published the following news story, part of which is presented below. (The paragraph structure and the use of bold is kept faithful to the original layout.)

Extract 4.1

> **Syria 'near miss' prompts US-Russia air safety talks**
>
> **The US and Russia are to hold new talks on air safety in Syria after it emerged combat aircraft from both nations came within miles of each other on Saturday.**
>
> The planes were in visual contact with each other, 10 to 20 miles (15–30km) apart, a US defence spokesman told reporters in Washington DC.
>
> It will be the third round of talks as the two countries seek to find ways of avoiding an accidental conflict. [...]

The important 5 Ws in the lead sentence are reported to give readers a clear sense of the story emerging in the Middle East and confirm factual details of events that could have escalated into a more serious situation:

who? US and Russia
what? near miss
where? Syria
when? Saturday (10th October 2015)
why? war

The striking *near miss* headline communicates the reason for reporting events that did not happen, where no-one was killed, and where no conflict escalated in the context of the Middle East crisis. This report may appear odd as readers would expect to be presented with stories that convey facts with far reaching consequences rather than events that did not occur or were avoided. Another near miss headline in Extract 4.2 appeared in the *MailOnline*, a digital version of the tabloid *Daily Mail* newspaper:

Extract 4.2

16 February 2014

Near miss! Motorised paraglider narrow avoids crashing into packed EasyJet passenger plane by only 150ft... and air traffic control failed to spot it

- **The Airbus A319 missed the flying-machine by only 150ft**
- **Pilot relayed the incident to air traffic control**
- **Kits to build the flying machines can be purchased online for around £1,500**
- **Aspiring pilots can start taking to the skies without any training**

An airliner that was coming in to land had a near miss in mid-air with a motorised parachutist at 2,000ft about the ground.

The Airbus A319 missed the flying-machine by only 150ft, causing the pilot to see the parachute canopy flash by the cockpit of the plane. [...]

Extract 4.2 presents a more detailed report of the facts to provide a summary of events. It also uses evaluative punctuation such as the exclamation mark to convey the reporter and newspaper's stance. Ellipsis, the omission of words and clauses, is shown with the three full stops between clauses to signal a gap but still conveys information by its very absence. Readers are left to fill in the missing details in the headlines to imagine what might have been. Further factual information is summarised in a bullet point layout under the headlines and emphasised in bold. Again, the news agency has reported events that were averted: in both scenarios, neither planes collided. Two more examples of headlines and excerpts about near misses are presented in Extracts 4.3 and 4.4 to exemplify that disnarrated news stories are pervasive:

Extract 4.3

BBC news online (11 May 2015)

Minute from disaster: What caused near catastrophe on the railway?

There has not been much about it in the media, but at the beginning of March Britain was less than a minute away from what might have been one of the country's worst train crashes.

In euphemistic railway speak, it was ranked as a 25 SPAD at SN45.

To you and me, a charter steam train carrying hundreds of leisure passengers ran through a red light approaching a junction on a main line, about a minute after an express train had gone through at about 70mph.

The close call happened just before 17:30 on Saturday 7 March at a junction in Wootton Bassett, Wiltshire.

Extract 4.4

Mail Online
Drone collision scare at Heathrow: Airbus in near miss with craft that ghosted into Britain's biggest airport undetected by air traffic control

- **The incident was rated as among the most serious near-collisions**
- **Pilot spotted the drone at 700ft - air traffic control radars had missed it**
- **It comes amid growing concerns about drones being flown by amateurs**
- **Sales of drones costing £35 to £3,350 have jumped ahead of Christmas**

By Mail on Sunday Reporter
Published: 7 December 2014

Near misses are not the only disnarrated events reported as news stories as Extract 4.5 from the guardian.com website shows:

Extract 4.5

Guardian online
Friday 20 September 2013

US nearly detonated atomic bomb over North Carolina – secret document

Exclusive: Journalist uses Freedom of Information Act to disclose 1961 accident in which one switch averted catastrophe

A secret document, published in declassified form for the first time by the Guardian today, reveals that the US Air Force came dramatically close to detonating an atom bomb over North Carolina that would have been 260 times more powerful than the device that devastated Hiroshima.

The document, obtained by the investigative journalist Eric Schlosser under the Freedom of Information Act, gives the first conclusive evidence that the US was narrowly spared a disaster of monumental proportions when two Mark 39 hydrogen bombs were accidentally dropped over Goldsboro, North Carolina on 23 January 1961 [...]

Extract 4.6 is an online news report (with a video that is widely available on the internet) about a terrorist attack at a church in Normandy, France.

Extract 4.6

EXPRESS

'I could have killed them all' Sky News reporter slated over bizarre terrorism report

> SKY NEWS reporter Martin Brunt has been blasted by viewers following a bizarre news report about the security of churches in the UK.
>
> By NEELA DEBNATH
> PUBLISHED: 19:16, Thu, Jul 28, 2016 | UPDATED: 20:54, Thu, Jul 28, 2016
>
> The crime correspondent was speaking outside a church in the wake of the tragedy in Normandy, France in which a priest was killed by a group of armed men.
>
> Following the tragedy, there have been calls to increase security on British churches to avoid any repeat attacks, and Martin went along to one to see how secure it was.
>
> The journalist told viewers: "The service began about 20 minutes ago and there are no obvious signs of any security, in fact this sign at the church door says, 'everybody is welcome'."
>
> He then walked into the building to survey the scene inside before coming back out and telling viewers: "There are about a dozen worshippers in there and one priest. If I was a terrorist, I could have killed them all."

The utterance 'If I was a terrorist, I could have killed them all' asks audiences to imagine a counterfactual scenario. The statement expresses the antinarratable in the form of a hypothetical condition using *if+could* and although left unsaid, the ellipted and negated 'but I didn't' or 'but I wasn't a terrorist' is nonetheless inferred in the context of this story. Disnarrated news stories that describe events with terrible consequences that *could have happened* such as the near miss examples above are numerous and present a subcategory of news that fulfils a further criteria of news values in addition to those proposed by Galtung and Ruge (1965) and Bell (1991). I suggest that there is a place for this dimension of storytelling in the news and add *THE DISNARRATED* to Table 4.2 as an additional news value to increase Bell's original list to thirteen. Disnarration here describes events that *could have happened* with serious consequences at a personal, national or international level.

Table 4.2 News values including the disnarrated (adapted from Bell 1991)

News value	*Description*
NEGATIVITY	Bad or negative
RECENCY	Has only just happened
DISNARRATED	**Could have happened**
PROXIMITY	Took place geographically close to the reader or viewer
CONSONANCE	Fits readers' or viewer's preconceptions or stereotypes about how the world is
UNAMBIGUITY	Is relatively clear-cut and unambiguous
UNEXPECTEDNESS	Is rare, unexpected or unpredictable
SUPERLATIVENESS	Is outstanding or superlative in some respect
RELEVENCE	Can be presented as relevant to the audience's own lives or experience
PERSONALISATION	Can be pictured in personal terms
ELITENESS	Involves news actors who are socially prominent in some respect
ATTRIBUTION	Comes from news sources who carry some kind of socially validated authority
FACTICITY	Consists of or can be supported by facts and figures

Disnarrated news stories, constituted by terms, phrases, and passages that consider what does not happen, exemplify Prince's (1988: 2) 'The elements in a narrative that explicitly consider and refer to what does not take place ("X didn't happen"; "Y could have happened but didn't")' as each example 'covers all the events that do not happen but, nonetheless, are referred to' (Prince 2003: 22). Prince (1988: 4) however, argues that disnarration 'has no role in news stories' because narratives are about 'assurance' because something happened rather than something did not and as such affects the narrativity of the story. Realized events are implicit in the criteria of *RECENCY* (has only just happened) and examples of news stories presented in this chapter (as well as others published widely) confirm that disnarrated news events are nevertheless newsworthy and relevant. Disnarrated events convey possible outcomes that could be serious (similar to those experiences narrated by children in the previous chapter where real danger was a likely consequence) and audiences are able to understand and makes sense of possible and negative outcomes, which may also have an impact on their lives. This point is explored further in the next part of the chapter.

Disnarration in news stories function to highlight some kind of breach—as with conventional news stories—but the reporting of this dimension of events appear to act as a foregrounding device

(Mukařovsky 1964 [1932]) because readers are expected to participate in interpreting the uses of negation and textual gaps to make sense of the text. In cognitive terms, negation 'involves some comparison between a real situation lacking some particular element and an imaginal situation that does not lack it' (Lawler 2010: 554) and in news stories, they generate scenarios with alternative outcomes of what could have happened. Events are reported with the knowledge that readers can infer the devastating consequences had the chain of events actually followed through, that is, the planes had crashed triggering greater conflict in the Middle East, or the paraglider and EasyJet passenger plane had collided leading to many deaths, or the nuclear bomb had detonated over the US etc. Newsworthiness is manifested in the interaction between the text and the audience, described as audience identification. The agenda for audience identification relies on the news values of *NEGATIVITY* (where bad or negative events are reported), *RELEVANCE* (where the story is relevant to the audience's own lives or experiences) and *PERSONALISATION* (where events in the story can be pictured in personal terms). Audience identification is possible because readers understand 'an alternative, a set of possible directions' (Prince 1988: 4), and can imagine the counterfactual projected by the *what if*? especially when imagined in personal terms.

To give an example of where *PERSONALISATION* is a hugely influential factor of how individuals assess counterfactual possibilities, Markman and McMullen (2014) highlight the case of a 2003 news article by the Associated Press with the news headline 'No 9-11 Compensation for Flight Attendant'. The article refers to Flight Attendant Kim Stroka, who avoided being killed on United Airlines Flight 93, one of four hijacked aircraft on 11 September, 2001, as she traded shifts with a co-worker who died when the plane crashed. Knowing she could have died, Stroka was unable to work and tried to claim medical disability payments for emotional distress. However, she was unsuccessful in her claim as the Court maintained nothing had actually happened to her. Stroka's experience is exceptional but this example illustrates how audiences can personalise negative events through counterfactual thinking with (lasting) traumatic effects as they are able to visualise themselves involved in traumatic events. The counterfactual scenarios presented in all the news extracts allows for speculation on how things could have been but audiences can rest assured that as the event has already occurred there is no possibility of the negative alternative outcome. Another example of counterfactual thinking is given by Hansen (2016: 130) who illustrates the journalist's speculation in the following:

> If the government, on the other hand, had been capable of dampening the overheating, the current increase in the unemployment would have been curbed at a lower peak than the level it is heading towards now.

The use of the third conditional structure beginning with the *If* clause + *would* + *present perfect* is used to communicate criticism or regret for events that did not take place. It also conveys the journalist's evaluative stance (Riddle Harding 2007) for a preferred outcome. Hansen's example is similar to the *what if* structure in children's disnarrated personal narratives (discussed in Chapter 3) as both disnarrated news events and children's personal narratives report events from a safe (temporal) distance, speculating on what could have happened (but did not).

The Discourse of News Values and Disnarration

A framework for understanding news values and how they are constructed is offered by Bednarek and Caple (2014) through corpus linguistic research on news discourse. Bednarek and Caple (2014: 135) argue that news values '*exist in and are constructed through discourse*' and that news is sold to its readers through linguistic choices rather than on the process and selection of news. Based on this premise, and drawing on an earlier study (Bednarek 2006), their framework offers a systematic and comprehensive analysis of the language of news discourse that adapts the list developed by Galtung and Ruge (1965) and Bell (1991). In their study, Bednarek and Caple identified the top 100-word frequency based on a 70,000 word corpus of British news discourse which was categorised into a list of nine news values with headings focusing on the linguistic features of news, including *NEGATIVITY, TIMELIMESS, PROXIMITY SUPERLATIVENESS* and *CONSONANCE*. Bednarek and Caple's (2014) framework can offer additional insights into the construction of disnarrated news and is applied to the short news Extracts 4.1–4.6 presented earlier in this chapter. A simplified version of Bednarek and Caple's (2014) list of news values with a summary of the key linguistic devices against each is presented in Table 4.3.

Table 4.3 The language of news discourse for the construction of news values (adapted from Bednarek and Caple 2014)

News value	*Description of linguistic devices*
NEGATIVITY	Negative evaluative language; negative emotions; negative lexis
TIMELINESS	Explicit reference to present, recent past, future, season; verb tense/aspect
PROXIMITY	Reference to place, nation, community; inclusive we and our pronouns
SUPERLATIVENESS	Quantifiers; intensifiers/intensified lexis; comparative and superlatives; repetition; metaphors and similes that intensify or quantify
ELITENESS	Labels/descriptions denoting high status/importance of individuals, organisations, nations involved
IMPACT	Evaluative language relating to impact of event; significant/relevant consequences (hypotheses, speculations, consequences, cause and effect relations)
NOVELTY	Evaluative language expressing newness, unexpectedness, unusual, comparison with other events in past; surprise
PERSONALISATION	Specific reference to emotions; quotes from ordinary people and references to ordinary individuals; eye witness reports
CONSONANCE	Language conveying expectedness; comparison with other past events; conventionalised metaphors; stereotypes; archetypes

An analysis of the news headlines and story in Extracts 4.1–4.6 reveal that they are constructed through three main news values: *NEGATIVITY*, *SUPERLATIVENESS* and *IMPACT*—see Table 4.4. Specific stylistic markers to convey ***negation***, ***comparators***, ***hypotheses***, ***speculations*** and ***consequences*** (which are also the linguistic features identified as communicating disnarration in children's personal experiences) confirm there is a discourse of disnarration.

Disnarrated events in the news have a valid place in society because they share reports about extraordinary events in the world we live in. In events that did not happen and might have been, newsworthiness is constructed in the imagination of the reader as much as through the linguistic choices in the text. As expected, the news value of *NEGATIVITY* or Trouble with a capital 'T' (Bruner 1997) appears to be the central theme common to disnarrated events to convey the important "bad news" or crisis central to a news story. Negativity guarantees a narrative that is tellable and worth sharing because there is a story to be told.

Table 4.4 The news values of *NEGATIVITY*, *SUPERLATIVENESS* and *IMPACT* and their linguistic expression in Extracts 4.1–4.6

Negativity	*Superlativeness*	*Impact*
Negative evaluative language; negative emotions; negative lexis	Quantifiers; intensifiers/intensified lexis; comparative and superlatives; repetition; metaphors and similes that intensify or quantify	Evaluative language relating to impact of event; significant/relevant consequences (hypotheses, speculations, consequences, cause and effect relations)
• accidental conflict • crashing into • failed to spot it • missed • near catastrophe • worst train crash • disaster • collision scare • ghosted into • missed it • catastrophe • devastated • disaster • detonated • killed • slated • bizarre • terrorism • armed men • attack • terrorist	• combat aircraft • third round of talks • by only 150 ft (also repeated) • packed EasyJet passenger plane • missed the flying machine (repeated) • without any training • minute from disaster • less than a minute away • hundreds of leisure passengers • Britain's biggest airport • the most serious near collision • Exclusive • dramatically close • accidentally dropped • 260 times more powerful than • secret document • conclusive evidence • monumental proportions • Freedom of Information Act (repeated) • armed men	• came within miles of each other • near miss • avoiding an accidental conflict • Near miss! • narrow avoids crashing • missed the flying machine • 150 ft… (use of ellipsis punctuation) • near catastrophe • close call • what might have been • averted catastrophe • nearly detonated • accident • narrowly spared a disaster • If I was a terrorist, I could have killed them all

References

Bednarek, M. (2006). *Evaluation in Media Discourse: Analysis of a Newspaper Corpus*. London: Continuum.

Bednarek, M., & Caple, H. (2014). Why Do News Values Matter? Towards a New Methodological Framework for Analysing News Discourse in Critical Discourse Analysis and Beyond. *Discourse and Society*, *25*(2), 135–158.

Bell, A. (1991). *The Language of News Media*. Oxford: Blackwell.

Bell, A. (1998). The Discourse Structure of News Stories. In A. Bell & P. Garrett (Eds.), *Approaches to Media Discourse* (pp. 64–104). Oxford: Blackwell.

Bruner, J. (1997). Labov and Waletzky Thirty Years On. *Journal of Narrative and Life History, 7*(1–4), 61–68.

Duszak, A. (1991). Schematic and Topical Categories in News Story Reconstruction. *Text, 11*, 503–522.

Evans, H. (1972). *Editing and Design: A Five-Volume Manual of English, Typography and Layout. Book One. Newsman's English*. London: Heinemann.

Galtung, J., & Ruge, M. H. (1965). The Structure of Foreign News: The Presentation of the Congo, Cuba and Cyprus in Four Norwegian Newspapers. *Journal of Peace Research, 2*(1), 64–90.

Hansen, K. R. (2016). News from the Future: A Corpus Linguistic Analysis of Future-Orientated, Unreal And Counterfactual News Discourse. *Discourse & Communication, 10*(2), 115–136.

Harcup, T. (2009). *Journalism, Principles and Practice* (2nd ed.). London: Sage.

Labov, W., & Waletzky, J. (1967). Narrative Analysis: Oral Versions of Personal Experience. In J. Holm (Ed.), *Essays on the Verbal and Visual Arts* (pp. 12–44). Seattle: University of Washington Press.

Lawler, J. (2010). Negation and Negative Polarity. In P. C. Hogan (Ed.), *Cambridge Encyclopedia of the Language Sciences* (pp. 554–555). Cambridge: Cambridge University Press.

Lule, J. (2001). *Daily News, Eternal Stories: The Mythological Role of Journalism*. New York: The Guilford Press.

Lutz, B., & Wodak, R. (1987). *Information für Informierte: Linguistische Studien zu Verständlichkeit und Verstehen von Hörfunknachrichten*. Vienna: Verlag der Österreichischen Akademie der Wissenschaften.

Markman, K. D., & McMullen, M. N. (2014). Reflective and Evaluative Modes of Mental Simulation. In D. R. Mandel, D. J. Hilton, & P. Catellani (Eds.), *The Psychology of Counterfactual Thinking* (pp. 77–93). London: Routledge.

Mukařovsky, J. (1964 [1932]). Standard Language and Poetic Language. In P. Garvin (Ed.), *A Prague School Reader on Aesthetics, Literary Structure and Style* (pp. 17–30). Washington, DC: Georgetown University Press.

Niblock, S. (2005). Practice and Theory: What Is News? In R. Keeble (Ed.), *Print Journalism, A Critical Introduction*. London: Routledge.

Prince, G. (1988). The 'Disnarrated'. *Style, 22*(1), 1–8.

Prince, G. (2003). *Dictionary of Narratology*. Lincoln and London: University of Nebraska Press.

Riddle Harding, J. (2007). Evaluative Stance and Counterfactuals in Language and Literature. *Language and Literature, 16*(3), 263–280.

Spencer-Thomas, O. (2005). *News Values* [online]. http://www.owenspencer-thomas.com/journalism/newsvalues. Accessed 12 November 2017.

Toolan, M. J. (2001). *Narrative: A Critical Linguistic Introduction* (2nd ed.). London: Routledge.

CHAPTER 5

Disnarration and the Unmentioned in Fiction

Abstract This chapter explores the dimension of disnarration and counterfactual divergence as unconventional storytelling modes in three fictional texts for insights of *what did not happen* and *what might have been*. The three fictional texts presented for analysis are two literary works of fiction: John Fowles's novel *The French Lieutenant's Woman*; Tobias Wolff's (1996) short story *Bullet in the Brain*; and the 2016 film *La La Land* directed by Damien Chazelle. The texts are analysed for their innovative narratological, literary and stylistic strategies, including plot divergences and forked pathways that generate alternative scenarios and unexpected plot twists. Marked uses of negation where absences simultaneously convey the less satisfactory version of a state of affairs at the same time as revealing the preferred version is also discussed for their linguistic form and purpose. There are also insights into how characters, through their own volition, trigger counterfactual scenarios to show that in their storyworld they are able to make choices when presented with a network of plot options.

Keywords Negation · Counterfactual divergence · Forked paths · Disnarration · Metalepsis · Mind-style · Metafiction · Fiction · Film · Short story

M. Lambrou, *Disnarration and the Unmentioned in Fact and Fiction*,
https://doi.org/10.1057/978-1-137-50778-5_5

'narrative is the one and only discourse that can portray consciousness'. Fludernik (1996: 27)

Introduction: Disnarration in Fiction

The previous two chapters explored disnarration (Prince 1988) in factual texts and looked specifically at the oral narratives of personal experience shared by children and also at media news stories to examine the phenomenon and relevance of *what did not happen* and *what might have been*. Analysis of both genres of factual texts provides insights into the discourse of disnarration that describes how the hypothetical *what if*? scenarios function by inviting audiences to notice negated, counterfactual and unrealized situations and imagine alternative outcomes. The use of negation generates what Leech (1983: 101) calls *negative uninformativeness*, where unrealized events are foregrounded because they require greater processing and are marked stylistically for this reason. This chapter turns to fictional texts to examine disnarration as a dimension of narrative storytelling to explore some of the unconventional techniques that convey *what did not happen* and *what might have been*. The chapter focuses on two literary texts and one film for the creative use of disnarration through forked pathways generating counterfactual alternatives and the startling use of negation to present idealised versions of a state of affairs. The texts discussed in this chapter are: John Fowles's novel *The French Lieutenant's Woman*; Tobias Wolff's (1996) short story *Bullet in the Brain*; and the 2016 film *La La Land* directed by Damien Chazelle. In all three texts, disnarration in the plot structure appears to be directly connected to, and a consequence of, characterization which may be at odds with the audience's expectations as *what does not happen* is used as a foregrounded plot device that is likely to 'disrupt a readers' pre-existing story 'schemata' (Lambrou 2019). This is certainly true where there are deeply embedded expectations of the idealised happy ending associated with conventional Victorian style novels, Hollywood romantic comedies and the final memories of a dying man.

John Fowles's *The French Lieutenant's Woman*

Fowles's (1969) *The French Lieutenant's Woman* is set in the mid-nineteenth century and written in the style of a fictional nineteenth century Victorian novel. The story is set in Lyme Regis, West Dorset and centres on three protagonists, whose lives intersect with dire consequences. The characters are the enigmatic Sarah Woodruff, the woman in the title; her admirer and subsequently her lover, Charles Smithson, a gentleman; and Charles's fiancée, the young and wealthy Ernestina Freeman. The novel features a number of literary techniques to narrate the story and gives the novel its metafictive dimension. The unconventional plot structure that offers then disnarrates more than one ending categorises the novel genre as postmodern despite its setting in Victorian times with a literary style that reflects writing of that period.

While Sarah, Charles and Ernestina are the main characters in the novel, it could be argued that there is a fourth major character in the form of the narrator, whose intrusive comments throughout the novel undermine the plot progression and fates of the characters in the storyworld—the diegesis. The unconventional storytelling mode is achieved through different types or levels of narration or 'narrative situation' (Stanzel 1986). The novel at first appears to have a heterodiegetic, third person narrator who is outside the diegesis and so can also be described as the extradiegetic narrator. Being outside the storyworld, the omniscient narrator has an overview of the plot and knowledge of characters' thoughts, feelings and motivations, all of which cannot be achieved by a first-person narrator. However, in *The French Lieutenant's Woman* there are sudden shifts in the narratorial situation when the narrator shifts out into the readers' discourse-world and addresses readers directly with evaluative comments on the characters and plot. The deliberate transgression between narrative levels is described by Genette (1980 [1972]: 234–235) as 'metalepsis' defined as 'any intrusion by the extradiegetic narrator or narratee into the diegetic universe (or by diegetic characters into a metadiegetic universe, etc.), or the inverse'. The effect is that readers are made to feel complicit in the plotting of the story. A further metafictive technique is used in *The French Lieutenant's Woman* when readers discover that the mysterious unnamed character who suddenly appears in the story and is critical of Charles's disobedient actions, is in fact the narrator, who asks:

> Now the question I am asking as I stare at Charles...what the devil am I going to do with you? (Ch. 55, p. 389)

The narrator is thought to be the author Fowles's not only because of the opinions expressed but because of the physical resemblance of the mysterious character to Fowles's who possesses 'a massively bearded face' and aged 'of forty or so' (Ch. 55, p. 387). The insertion of the narrator as a character into the storyworld is described as 'author metalepsis', when 'an author (or his reader) introduces himself into the fictive action of the narrative' (Genette 1988 [1983]: 88). Through metalepsis and author metalepsis, the narration changes to homodiegetic, first-person or I-narrator that self-reflexively considers the fictionality of plot structure by reminding readers the novel is a work of fiction. For example, with asides such as 'having brought this fiction to a thoroughly traditional ending' (Ch. 45, p. 327) the ensuing plot twists and counterfactual endings are made much more plausible because metafiction is open to a whole range of plot digressions. The most famous feature of the novel is the three endings, outlined below (see Lambrou 2019).

> *Ending 1.* Charles and Ernestina marry though it is not a particularly happy marriage but it conforms to expectations of the literary genre. Sarah is forgotten;
>
> *Ending 2.* Charles and Sarah meet some years later in London where Sarah is living and Charles is told of their child. There is some hope that the relationship may rekindle;
>
> *Ending 3.* Same events as in *Ending 2* up to the point of Charles and Sarah meeting some years later in London. Instead, the final meeting between them does not go well as Sarah wants her independence and she rejects Charles. Charles leaves feeling angry at having been manipulated and is unaware of their child.

(Audiences of the 1981 film adaptation of *The French Lieutenant's Woman* directed by Karel Reisz will only be aware of two endings.)

The first of the plot twists occurs two thirds of the way through the novel when the third person narration pauses and the narrator speaks directly to readers to describe the first of three endings for Sarah, Charles and Ernestina. The first ending culminates in the marriage between Ernestina and Charles, and so provides a conventional ending expected in a Victorian novel:

> And so the story ends. What happened to Sarah, I do not know – whatever it was, she never troubled Charles again... Charles and Ernestina did not live happily ever after; but they lived together. (Ch. 44, pp. 4–325)

The traditional (not-so) happy ending is also an example of the para-narratable or what would not be told because of literary convention (Warhol 2005, 2010, 2013). In Victorian fiction, it would be improbable for Charles and his lover, Sarah, to be together in this genre of fiction. In the next chapter, Chapter 45, the opening paragraph reveals that the marriage just described is an imagined scenario, dreamt by Charles and dismissed by the narrator:

> having brought this fiction to a thoroughly traditional ending, I had better explain that although I have described in the last two chapters happened, it did not happen quite in the way you were led to believe ... the last few pages you have read are not what happened but what he spent the hours between London and Exeter imagining what might happen. (Ch. 45, p. 327)

This false scenario is disnarrated through the use of negation with 'it did not happen' and 'are not what happened' offered as part of the narrator's explanation (emphasised in italics, below):

> having brought this fiction to a thoroughly traditional ending, I had better explain that although I have described in the last two chapters happened, *it did not happen* [*disnarration*] quite in the way you were led to believe ... the last few pages you have read *are not what happened* [*disnarration*] but what he spent the hours between London and Exeter imagining what might happen. (Ch. 45, p. 327)

The use of negation is linguistically marked as the expected outcome between and engaged couple is marriage but what is foregrounded is the opposite. The idealised and positive version of events are subverted because Charles is able to speculate on an imagined future with Ernestina, make his own decisions and break off his engagement to pursue Sarah. Fowles's as author-narrator goes as far as to blame his characters for their actions. He claims that Charles, Ernestina and Sarah are able to choose their own fates and are not under the control of the author. Earlier in Chapter 13, the author-narrator describes his inability to control his characters who must also have their 'freedom' and have agency:

> It is only when our characters and events begin to disobey us that they begin to live. When Charles left Sarah on her cliff-edge, I ordered him to

> walk straight back to Lyme Regis. But he did not; he gratuitously turned and went down to the Dairy. (Ch. 13, p. 98)

Fowles's characters are given a semi-autonomous existence that is integral to the context of the story. Paradoxically, the very presence of a narrator asserting his characters' independence from his control somewhat undermines their total freedom of choice because he also allows them to follow their wishes. Nevertheless, the ability to make choices echoes Bremond and Cancalon's (1980) 'network of possibilities' where choices open up alternative pathways, that is, whether Charles decides to stay with Ernestina or decides to leave. *Ending 1* is the first of the counterfactual endings as Fowles's tricks the reader with the unnarratable 'what might have been and yet is not' (Warhol 2010: 46).

In the second and third endings in Chapters 60 and 61, Charles and Sarah meet some years later and discuss the prospect of their future together. In the time that has elapsed, Sarah has had Charles's baby but he is unaware of his child. Charles is told of the child and Sarah accepts Charles's offer to spend their future lives together (Ch. 60). The third ending uses the device of author metalepsis as the author-narrator again becomes a physical presence in the diegesis and observes Charles from afar. In an effort to disrupt events by intervening, the author-narrator turns his wristwatch back by 15 minutes so generating an alternative pathway: the same scene of the meeting with Sarah is re-enacted however, in Ending 3, Sarah rejects Charles's offer of marriage, resulting in Charles awakening 'to the reality of the situation' (Ch. 61, p. 443). The result is that Charles leaves angrily, unaware of his child with Sarah. Dannenberg (2008: 2) argues that the forked path structure or divergence created by 'the bifurcation or branching of narrative paths' allows characters and plot to take alternative paths and for characters to reflect and evaluate their situations so that options and narrative ways exist in the storyworld as they do in the real world. In *The French Lieutenant's Woman*, counterfactual divergences are triggered by both the heterodiegetic narrator 'creating the emotional undertones of an observer who seems to be on the same level as the character' (Dannenberg 2008: 123) and Charles, a wayward character making his own decisions. We are told of Charles's bitterness and the 'tears in his eyes' and told that he may be walking towards 'an imminent self-given death?'. Readers are also told 'he has at last found an atom of faith in himself, his true uniqueness' as he is left to contemplate both his and Sarah's actions in a process of counterfactual thinking to understand past mistakes and the causal factors that led to them (Roese and Olson 1995). Charles is unable to change past mistakes and his counterfactual thinking in the final Chapter 61 effectively describes how 'People may strategically generate representations of how things could have been in order to make themselves or others feel better' (p. 174). He can only project what his future might be:

> It meant a return to America; it meant thirty-four years of struggling upwards – all in vain, in vain, in vain, all height lost: it meant, of this he was sure, a celibacy of the heart as total as hers. (Ch. 61, p. 444)

Charles's emotions come to the fore but instead of his 'struggling upward' to convey regret through the construction of an upward counterfactual for an improved version of his future reality (Dannenberg 2008: 120), readers are given a glimpse of the hardship he will face as he contemplates 'a less plausible ending to their story' (Fowles's 1969: 445). The three endings for Charles, Sarah and Ernestina cannot exist at the same time and in the same space. Opting for one automatically disnarrates the other two plot outcomes as if they were never imagined or existed. In terms of which outcome is the best for Charles and Sarah, the third ending reflects the true selves of the protagonists based on their characterization and motivations and critics have felt it to be the most realistic of all three outcomes (Scruggs 1985: 96); so there could be no other ending.

Bullet in the Brain: Negation as Disnarration

In this section, the discussion on disnarration focuses on a short story by the American author Tobias Wolff entitled *Bullet in the Brain*. The short story first appeared in *The New Yorker* (on September 25, 1995) and was later published in a collection of short stories called *The Night in Question* (1996). As a short piece of prose fiction, *Bullet in the Brain* is expected to uphold certain characteristics associated with the genre, such as 'a degree of mystery, elision, uncertainty' (Hanson 1989: 25). It should also fulfil Poe's claim that a short story can be read in one sitting. The literary theorist Mary Louise Pratt (1994) offers eight points to describe the 'dependent relationship' between a novel and short story with the first four being propositions describing the incompleteness with respect to the novel while the last four stating characteristics that are related to the short story's status as 'a lesser genre' than the novel:

Proposition 1. *The novel tells a life, the short story tells a fragment of a life*
Proposition 2. *The short story deals with a single thing, the novel with many things*
Proposition 3. *The short story is a sample, the novel is the whole hog*
Proposition 4. *The novel is the whole text, the short story is not*
5. Subject matter
6. Orality
7. Narrative traditions
8. Craft versus art.

(See Pratt 1994: 99–109)

The brevity of the short story telling format may leave readers needing to fill in details of plot and characterization to build on and make sense of events which might be compromised (i.e. ellipted) by the reduced word length. As Abbott (2013: 136) explains:

> Where the novel with its greater length, sequentiality, and detail can build up an autonomous world in which the reader feels at home, the short story has a "poetic" density, so that a single image can dominate our understanding, tying together themes and incidents.

The 'single image' dominating readers' mind can be made sense of by 'tying together themes and incidents' which are scattered in the story as clues. Pieced together like a jigsaw, they can provide a satisfying "whole", a narrative that readers can enjoy, interpret and understand despite the condensed storytelling form.

Bullet in the Brain is narrated in the third person by an extradiegetic narrator and concerns Anders, 'a book critic known for the weary, elegant savagery with which he dispatched almost everything he reviewed' (p. 200). One afternoon, Anders visits the bank and while waiting in a queue to be served, two armed robbers enter the bank and attempt to rob it. Despite everyone being ordered to keep their mouth shut as the robbers make their demands, Anders is unable to stop himself from criticising the style of language uttered by the robbers, all within their earshot. Anders is particularly amused by their use of clichéd expressions associated with the speech of archetypal baddies that he describes as being "Right out of 'The Killers'" (p. 202) such as: "you're all dead meat" (p. 201), "Bright boy!" (p. 202), "You think you can fuck with me?" (p. 203) and "Fuck with me again, you're history. *Capiche*?" (p. 203). Even after several threats from the robbers and with a pistol jammed under his chin, Anders is still not able to control himself and responds to the robber's "Capiche" with a burst of laughter and "I'm sorry, I'm sorry," then snorted helplessly through his fingers and said, "*Capiche* – oh, God, *capiche*" (p. 203). The robber shoots Anders in the head. The story does not end there. In Anders's final moments as the bullet travels through his brain, readers are taken on a journey along with the bullet and told of his long-forgotten memories 'as his life passed before his eyes' (p. 204) until reaching Anders's final, unexpected memory.

As a short story, ***Bullet in the Brain*** appears to adhere to many of the characteristics proposed by Pratt (1994: 99–101), above, for example, 'Proposition 1. *The novel tells a life, the short story tells a fragment of a life*'. Otherwise described as a 'moment of truth' short stories describe 'a single point of crisis in the life of a central character' that is often life changing. ***Bullet in the Brain*** does indeed narrate a life changing episode in Anders's life but uses disnarration creatively to tell of the many significant events in his life, paradoxically, during his dying moments. The 'fragment of a life' is explored further in the second 'Proposition 2. *The short story deals with a single thing, the novel with many things*', that is made more shocking as Anders's murder takes place during a routine visit to the bank on an ordinary day with an outcome that no-one could have predicted. Or could they?

In terms of story structure, ***Bullet in the Brain*** is composed of two parts roughly equal in word length with the first part narrating the visit to the bank and events leading to the shooting, and the second part describing what happened after the shooting and Anders's final moments up to his death. After the shooting, readers are given a detailed forensic description of the bullet's trajectory through Anders's brain and the devastating injury to flesh and bone. The description of the bullet's damage as it passes through is lexically rich with words belonging to the semantic field of medicine to conjure up a graphic description of the impact of the shooting and bullet which 'smashed Anders's skull': 'brain', 'bone', 'the cerebral cortex', 'the corpus callosum', 'the basal ganglia', and 'the thalmus' (pp. 203–204). The juxtaposition of the comedic tone of the first part of the short story is an effective device as the dramatic change to a crime genre is unexpected. The same paragraph that describes the devastation to Anders's brain also makes the first reference to a long-forgotten memory that will be recalled in the final sentences of the short story, 'flukishly calling to life a summer afternoon some forty years past' (p. 204) and functions to prime readers for the final dénouement.

The descriptions of life events and their disnarration appear in the next paragraph and is framed with 'It is worth noting what Anders did not remember, given what he did remember' (p. 204). This is a curious sentence as the expectation is that Anders would remember significant memories 'flashing before his eyes'. What follows instead is a series of notable but forgotten memories which are systematically presented over the next three paragraphs. Up to this point, the narrative events are temporally ordered but this sequence pauses to allow for an anachronistic shift in time to earlier points in Anders's life to describe the various forgotten memories over his lifetime, including:

> He did not remember his first lover, Sherry… (p. 204)
> Anders did not remember his wife… (p. 204)
> He did not remember standing outside his daughter's door… (p. 204)
> Anders did not remember his dying mother… (p. 204)
> Nor did Anders remember seeing a woman leap to her death… (p. 205)
> He did not remember shouting, "Lord have mercy!"… (p. 205)
> He did not remember deliberately crashing his father's car into a tree… (p. 205)

Instead, what Anders did remember in his final memory is revealed to be a minor event from his childhood some forty years earlier. Readers are told, 'This is what he remembered' (p. 205):

> Heat. A baseball field. Yellow grass, the whirr of insects, himself leaning against a tree as the boys of the neighborhood gather for a pickup game […] Then the last two boys arrive, Coyle and a cousin of his from Mississippi. Anders has never met Coyle's cousin before and will never see him again […] and someone asks the cousin what position he wants to play. "Shortstop," the boy says. "Short's the best position they is".

The final epiphany delivers an unexpected plot twist that is likely to disrupt expectations because it is so unremarkable when compared to the extraordinary experiences in Anders's life. Yet this final memory provides a useful insight into Anders's character because we learn that even as a child, he is 'roused, elated' (p. 206) by the boy's non-standard use of grammar and unexpectedness, a detail that refers back to his work as a book critic where words choices are central to a book's success or failure.

Stylistically, the forgotten memories are disnarrated through negation which 'covers all the events that *do not* happen but, nonetheless, are referred to (in a negative or hypothetical mode) by the narrative text' (Prince 1988: 2). The memories are foregrounded structurally through devices such as semantic parallelism (repeated meaning), lexical parallelism (repeated words) and grammatical parallelism (repeated clausal structures). The use of negation, reinforced in 41 lines of the text (across 16 sentences) and mostly following a structure of noun phrase (NP) + *did not remember* (negation) + clause is the most marked feature here to convey what was forgotten, e.g.:

> He (NP) + *did not remember* (negation) + his first lover, Sherry (clause)

There are also two examples that begin with negation using *none* and *nor*:

> None of these did he remember; not one. (204)
> Nor did Anders remember seeing a woman leap to her death… (205)

The use of negative clauses asserts that 'some event, situation, or state of affairs does not hold. Negative clauses usually occur in the context of some presupposition, functioning to negate or counter-assert that presupposition' (Payne 1997: 282). *Bullet in the Brain* deliberately plays with 'narrative expectation' (Toolan 2009: 113) by confusing rather than guiding readers' expectation of how the narrative progresses with its creative use of negative constructions. As Nahajec (2014: 119) explains, negated information is treated as if it is expected and 'these expectations can also be apparent in the co-text and context as well as projected through the process of negating'. The narrator persists in telling readers many unrecalled and often intimate events that fill the biographical gaps in Anders's life, outside the one central event narrated in the short story. By telling readers what Anders did not remember, readers are simultaneously told about Anders life and forced to notice what is forgotten. Negation here is a meaning-making resource as through communicating 'negative uninformativeness' (Leech 1983: 101) it draws attention to what does not take place and what does not take place is given as much emphasis as what does. In other words, 'the negatives in fact create what they negate' (Nørgaard 2007: 36) and this 'helps us to envisage both scenarios' (Jeffries and McIntyre 2010: 95). The use of negated propositions essentially foregrounds (and rejects) experiences that Anders is not conscious of against the one remembered memory.

In Text World Theory terms, negatives create textual sub-worlds where 'There are forms of negation [...] which not only delete an entity, but also introduce it at the same time' (Werth 1999: 253–254). Stockwell (2009: 34) explains that:

> A negation [...] creates a mental world-switch from the current text world into a world with a different ontological status. The hearer/reader's relationship to this embedded switched world is also experientially different. In order to process a negation, the reader must imagine—however temporarily or transiently—another world in which the state of affairs following the negation does exist; this sub-world is then tagged as being in a negational relationship with the text world. The crucial point here is that the reader has to hold the negated state in mind in order to negate it.

Negation cleverly invokes then revokes a proposition and creates a conceptual lacuna in the process suggesting 'a sense that there is not simply a space but something missing that was previously occupying the space' (Stockwell 2009: 35). Anders's experiences are explicitly referred to in a negative mode and then explicitly disnarrated using 'terms, phrases, and passages that consider what did not or does not take place' (Prince 1988: 3). Readers understand that Anders did experience the events that he does not remember as they happened during his life: they can only be forgotten because they occurred as real experiences.

The use of negation to disnarrate Anders's memories not only creates marked effects in the plot but simultaneously offers readers insights into Anders's complex character psychology. Characterization can be constructed through the linguistic choices or prompts in the text (bottom-up processing) but also drawn from the reader's own schematic knowledge (top-down processing) gained from knowledge of similar characters and genres encountered by the reader previously (Culpeper 2001). Characters can also be constructed by what is narrated not just in terms of the description of the character but through the linguistic choices to convey their experiences and expectations. Margolin (1990: 453) describes literary characters as verbal constructs, who in Western culture, are understood to be 'made up from words, textually identified by a referring expression, invented by an author for some purpose'. In *Bullet in the Brain*, character expectations are manipulated through the marked use of negation which 'reveal what is expected in a given situation and of a particular person' (Karttunen 2008: 419). The expectation is that Anders should have remembered significant life events and that these memories should have been articulated in the positive, for example: *Anders remembered his wife, He remembered standing outside his daughter's door, Anders remembered his dying mother.* I argue that the use of negation is entirely in keeping with Anders's character and that his forgotten memories reflect his *mind-style*, 'the distinctive linguistic representation of an individual mental self' (Fowler 1977: 103). Mind-style is achieved in the linguistic patterns formed by lexical and grammatical choices as well as through speech representation and can project a character's world view by providing insights into their ideologies, emotions, motivations and relationships through stylistic choices. Semino (2014: 155) suggests that:

> when a particular (linguistic) behaviour is foregrounded through 'deviation' from default or conventional expectations, a few instances of that behaviour may be sufficient to attribute a (mental) trait to a character, even though that character does not exhibit that behaviour consistently.

(For a broader discussions of mind style, see Gregoriou 2007; Semino 2002). To understand how the use of negation contributes to the textual construction of Anders, consider the many clues scattered throughout *Bullet in the Brain*: readers are told that Anders is a book critic in the first paragraph, 'known for the weary, elegant savagery with which he dispatched almost everything he reviewed' (p. 200). His sarcasm is evident in the brief interaction with other waiting customers in the queue and his scrutiny of language is vocalised when confronted by the robbers and their idiosyncratic speech style. Despite the dangerous situation, not just to himself but to the other customers, Anders finds their idiomatic expressions too absurd to be able to remain silent and reveals his evaluation of their language style rather expressively, to his detriment. The final piece of evidence is revealed after the shooting. The list of forgotten memories told through flashbacks at such a crucial point in his life also suggests a selfish and self-absorbed man whose favoured memory over and above the meaningful events in his life, is also related to the momentary use of non-standard language—by a child. Through the recreated biographical backstory of disnarrated memories, readers are given an understanding of who Anders is, what he has become, and significantly, why his untimely death in the bank that day was inevitable.

La La Land: Counterfactuality, Disnarration and the Forked (Motorway) Path

The final discussion on disnarration and what does not happen explores plot dimension in the 2016 film *La La Land*, written and directed by Damien Chazelle. The film is best described as a musical romantic comedy best known for an unexpected plot twist at the end of the film where a counterfactual ending of *what might have been* is generated between the leading protagonists. The film centres on the relationship between a jazz pianist, Sebastian (played by the actor Ryan Gosling) and aspiring actress Mia (played by Emma Stone). The story at first appears to follow the conventional romantic Hollywood film genre of *boy meets girl* and they fall in love after the usual series of hit-and-miss scenarios that have to be overcome. Audiences are immediately made aware that both characters are passionate about their careers and determined to succeed. However, it is not until the final part of the film that audiences see the sacrifices both have made to achieve their success in a flashforward of five years where it is revealed that Sebastian and Mia are not together. In the five years that have passed, Mia has become a famous film actress and is married to David, a man unknown to audiences up to this point in the film. They also have a child together. Meanwhile, Sebastian has become a successful musician and achieved his dream of owning a Jazz club, called *Sebs*. This is not the only plot twist. Chazelle uses a dimension of storytelling where counterfactual divergence—a forked path scenario (Borges 2000 [1944])—is generated by the protagonists and conceptualised metaphorically by the branching in two of a motorway. Readers are disorientated by the sudden shift in time and space, firstly by the anachronistic shift to the future and with a further plot twist, back to the very moment the counterfactual scenario is imagined, to disnarrate what *did not happen but might have been*. To explain, the plot jumps to five years in the future and in a last-minute change to their evening plans caused by severe traffic jams, audiences see Mia and David turn off on the motorway (a literal forked path) and find themselves walking into a Jazz club called *Sebs*. It is only after the couple have sat down and the entertainment starts that Mia realises the jazz pianist is her former lover, Sebastian. At the same moment, Sebastian sees Mia in the audience and their eyes meet. At this moment, there is a pause in the storyworld: both are suddenly transported into another dimension, a 'wish-world' (Fludernik 2009: 107), to a place where instead of having separated, Mia and Sebastian are a couple with a child in scenes that replicate earlier scenes of Mia and David together. Audiences are shown an idealised and domesticated life together in a *what might have been* state of affairs had Mia and Sebastian not separated. To recreate the idealised scenario, the imagined events are captured in a silent, sunlit home movie style of cinematography and given a dreamlike quality (see Lambrou 2018). The home movie is presented as a montage of short clips of Mia and Sebastian getting married, the birth of their child, the child's birthday etc. that Mia and Sebastian—as well as the audience—watch together in a further metafictive twist to the plot. This counterfactual representation of Mia and Sebastian's alternative existence causes another shift in the level of the storyworld where Mia and David's life could be viewed as their discourse world, that is, their real world, and the imagined Mia and Sebastian scenario as the text-world. Just as audiences begin to accept this turn of events, they are then shown Mia and Sebastian, in a last-minute change to their evening plans caused by severe traffic jams, turn off on the motorway (the literal forked path again) to find themselves walking into a Jazz club called *Sebs* in an exact and parallel telling of events. All of a sudden, the pianist becomes Sebastian, Mia is sitting beside her husband David, and Mia and Sebastian are back to the very moment they set eyes on each other. The counterfactual what *might have been* imagined by Mia and Sebastian is disnarrated as suddenly as it was imagined.

The counterfactual *what if*? scenario in *La La Land* is best described by Dannenberg (2008: 119) as 'a hypothetical alteration in a past sequence of events that changes the events in a factual sequence in order to create a different, counterfactual outcome'. As Mia and David exist at a point in the story before the alteration, the counterfactual scenario in the narrative is the *antecedent*, whereas Mia and Sebastian's imagined life after the point of the counterfactual divergence is the *consequence*. The counterfactual ending provides an example of what social psychologists refer to as 'counterfactual thoughts' that 'often focus prescriptively on what "should have been"'... 'that is, on what decisions or actions might have led directly to a more desired outcome and thus "ought" to have been implemented' (Roese and Olson 1996: 200).

The branching motorway in *La La Land* offers the metaphorical point of bifurcation that generates plot options to allow audiences to glimpse 'choices not made, the roads not taken, possibilities not actualized, goals not reached' (Prince 1992: 36). There are several other subtler points of divergence in *La La Land* in addition to the counterfactual scenario described above (and in a. below) where forked paths offer diversions that foreground the complexity of the narrative's hidden labyrinth of plot options. See b–d below:

a. The forked motorway plot pathway

Storyworld	Mia and her husband David are on their way to an event but are stuck in a traffic jam. They change plans and turn off the motorway (a literal forked path) to go to dinner instead and walk into Seb's Jazz club
Counterfactual scene	Mia and Sebastian never separated and the same scenes are replayed but with Sebastian instead of David

In the re-imagined life together or *what if*? montage, Mia and Sebastian's life replicates Mia and David's real life. They are also shown caught in a traffic jam, changing plans and turning off the same motorway that forks as they enact the same plot and find themselves in a Jazz club, taking them back to real time (their discourse world) and their real lives. In terms of characterization, 'Mia and David's sudden decision to change plans because of external circumstances (the traffic jam) is a further example of characters making choices as a result of having their own volition' (Lambrou 2018: 38).

b. The counterfactual first kiss

Storyworld	In an early scene, Mia is drawn into a jazz club by the music played by Sebastian. She sees Sebastian argue with the club's manager. Sebastian then storms out of the club, bumping into Mia as he exits
Counterfactual scene	In the *what if*? counterfactual scenario (shown in the film montage), the events in the jazz club are rewritten as Sebastian kisses Mia

The significance of the kiss in the counterfactual scene is that Mia and Sebastian establish their relationship earlier to live happily ever after compared to the actual events in the storyworld where there are several *boy meets girl then loses girl* plot of the romantic comedy genre. The hit-and-miss scenes are exemplified in c. and d. below which trigger a forking path. Interestingly, these events also take place on the motorway for the metaphorical representation of LIFE IS A JOURNEY (Lakoff and Johnson 1980). Texts c. and d. are taken from the *La La Land* film script. The emphasis in bold to highlight points in the plot that lead to the forking, is mine

c.
The cars stagger forward. Sebastian's car almost BUMPS into Mia's as **he changes lanes**. He and she see each other for a second -- before **their cars head their separate ways**.

With that - we follow Mia… (p. 3)

d.
EXT. 101 FREEWAY - EARLIER THAT MORNING

The same 101 traffic jam we began the movie with. This time, we're on Sebastian.

As we saw before, **he nearly bumps into Mia's car. Turns, then cuts out of traffic. Merges onto a more free-flowing freeway…** (p. 11)

La La Land's alternative ending is an example of the self-focused counterfactual (Dannenberg 2008) as the events leading to this scenario is a consequence of characters responding to events in their lives. The complex ontological structure of the *what if*? scenario invites audiences to make comparisons of the events—in the real and in the counterfactual worlds, that is:

> A counterfactual can perform an important authenticating function in the realist tradition: character-counterfactual speculations […] serve to strengthen the impression that the narrative world is "real" by constructing a further, contrastive "less real" sequence of events that reinforces the apparent reality of the narrative world by *ontological default*. (Dannenberg 2008: 54)

The imagined plot offered in *La La Land* is mimetic of the characters and their lives so it is easy to imagine that a happy ending between Mia and Sebastian would be the more desirable while also fulfilling the conventional Hollywood happy ending. While this may be the preferred outcome, I suggest that for the characters to feel "real", they need to follow separate paths:

> Because Mia and Sebastian's motivations have been established early in the film, *La La Land's* ending with both having pursued and chosen their dreams over their relationship provides the more satisfying conclusion if audiences accept that characters consider situations and have choices; they are not so much constructs but conscious beings in their storyworld with their own hopes, wishes and desires. (Lambrou 2018: 34)

It was always unlikely that Mia and Sebastian would remain together because their desire for individual success was far greater than their desire for each other. By ending their relationship to pursue their dreams, they remain true to their character even as constructs within the fictional narrative where they are presented as real as people in their discourse world. As Lindholm (2003: 208) explains, 'the disnarrated allows its readers to delve into the hopes, possible directions, dreams and fears of the focalized character' and in *La La Land*, audiences are given an opportunity to understand the interior feelings of its protagonists through this dimension of storytelling.

Counterfactual divergence which creates multiple versions of the story where characters are unaware of the other plot trajectory and alternative experiences is not an uncommon plot device. One well-known film is *Sliding Doors* (1998) where two timelines 'tells of the parallel lives of the protagonist, Helen, whose life splits into two parallel universes as a result of a 2-second delay when catching the train' (Lambrou 2018: 35, see Chapter 2 for a fuller discussion). Other popular stories with counterfactual plots have protagonists who are aware they have somehow stepped into another dimension and an altered plot and timeline, as in the classic film *It's a Wonderful Life* (1946) directed by Frank Capra. The protagonist George Bailey (played by James Stewart) 'finds himself in a downward counterfactual world where he was never born' (Lambrou 2018: 35). After his suicide attempt is stopped by his guardian Angel, Bailey finds his hometown has become unrecognisable and none of his friends know who he is. He has a number of nightmarish experiences and comes to realise how important his life had been and how many lives he touched with his generosity and numerous interventions. He begs for his former life and is taken back to his real life where everything is back to normal. Similarly, in *The Family Man* (2000), a modern-day Frank Capra story, the successful, single businessman Jack Campbell (played by Nicholas Cage) wakes up on Christmas Day to find himself married to his ex-girlfriend and the father of two children, in a parallel universe also triggered by an encounter with a stranger. In this dimension, Jack is given a glimpse of what his life could have been like had he married his girlfriend. With each day, he eventually comes to realise how much fuller and happier this alternative life could be compared to his reality but he is returned to his real life with no possibility of returning. Jack's counterfactual life is disnarrated as suddenly as it is conjured and he is left to try to somehow repair the point of divergence (the break-up with his ex-girlfriend many years earlier) back in his present. Dickens' (1843) *A Christmas Carol* also offers the miser Ebenezer Scrooge a *what might have been* scenario when he is confronted with his past, present and future through supernatural means and forced to evaluate what he has become because of choices made in his youth. Happily, it is not too late for Scrooge as these ghostly experiences transform him into a kinder, more generous man 'who possess[es] an emotional depth [and] a regret for lost opportunities' (Kelly 2003: 25–26).

References

Abbott, H. P. (2013). *Real Mysteries, Narrative and the Unknowable*. Columbus, OH: Ohio State University.

Borges, J. L. (2000 [1944]). The Garden of Forking Paths. In A. Hurley (Trans.), *Collected Fictions* (pp. 119–128). London: Penguin.

Bremond, C., & Cancalon, E. D. (1980). The Logic of Narrative Possibilities. *New Literary History, 11*(3), 387–411.

Culpeper, J. (2001). *Language and Characterisation: People in Plays and Other Texts*. London: Routledge.

Dannenberg, H. P. (2008). *Coincidence and Counterfactuality: Plotting Time and Space in Narrative Fiction*. Lincoln and London: University of Nebraska Press.

Dickens, C. (1843). *A Christmas Carol*. London: Chapman & Hall.

Fludernik, M. (1996). *Towards a 'Natural' Narratology*. London: Routledge.

Fludernik, M. (2009). *An Introduction to Narratology*. London: Routledge.

Fowler, R. (1977). *Linguistics and the Novel*. London: Methuen.

Fowles, J. (1969). *The French Lieutenant's Woman*. London: Vintage.

Genette, G. (1980 [1972]). *Narrative Discourse: An Essay on Method*. Ithaca, NY: Cornell University Press.

Genette, G. (1988 [1983]). *Narrative Discourse Revisited*. Ithaca, NY: Cornell University Press.

Gregoriou, C. (2007). *Deviance in Contemporary Crime Fiction*. Basingstoke: Palgrave.

Hanson, C. (1989). "Things Out of Words": Towards a Poetics of Short Fiction. In C. Hanson (Ed.), *Rereading the Short Story* (pp. 22–23). Houndmills: Macmillan.

It's a Wonderful Life. (1946). Directed by Frank Capra.

Jeffries, L., & McIntyre, D. (2010). *Stylistics*. Cambridge: Cambridge University Press.

Karttunen, L. (2008). A Sociostylistic Perspective on Negatives and the Disnarrated: Lahiri, Roy, Rushdie. *Partial Answers: Journal of Literature and the History of Ideas, 6*(2), 419–441.

Kelly, R. M. (2003). Introduction. In C. Dickens (Ed.), *A Christmas Carol* (pp. 9–30). Ontario: Broadway Press.

Lakoff, G., & Johnson, M. (1980). *Metaphors We Live By*. Chicago: The University of Chicago Press.

Lambrou, M. (2018). "*La La Land*": Counterfactuality, Disnarration and the Forked (Motorway) Path. In R. Page, B. Busse, & N. Nørgaard (Eds.), *Rethinking Language, Text and Context: Interdisciplinary Research in Stylistics in Honour of Michael Toolan* (pp. 29–42). London: Routledge.

Lambrou, M. (2019). Metalepsis, Counterfactuality and Being Led up the "Forked" Garden Path: 'Manipulating' Readers in Fiction. In S. Sorline (Ed.), *Stylistic Manipulation of the Reader in Contemporary Literature*. London: Bloomsbury.

Leech, G. (1983). *The Principles of Pragmatics*. Harlow: Longman.

Lindholm, H. (2003). Perhaps She Had Not Told Him All the Story: The Disnarrated in James Joyce's Dubliners. In F. Iftekharuddin, J. Boyden, M. Rohrberger, & J. Claudet (Eds.), *The Postmodern Short Story: Forms and Issues* (pp. 207–219). Westport, CT: Paeger.

Margolin, U. (1990). The What, the When, and the How of Being a Character in Literary Narrative. *Style, 24*(3), 453–468.

Nahajec, L. (2014). Negation, Expectation and Characterisation: Analysing the Role of Negation in Character Construction in *To Kill a Mockingbird* (Lee 1960) and *Stark* (Elton 1989). In S. Chapman & B. Clark (Eds.), *Pragmatic Literary Stylistics* (pp. 111–131). London: Palgrave Macmillan.

Nørgaard, N. (2007). Disordered Collarettes and Uncovered Tables: Negative Polarity as a Stylistic Device in Joyce's 'Two Gallants'. *Journal of Literary Semantics, 36*(1), 35–52.

Pratt, M. L. (1994). The Short Story: The Long and the Short of It. In C. E. May (Ed.), *The New Short Story Theories* (pp. 91–113). Columbus: Ohio University Press.

Prince, G. (1988). The 'Disnarrated'. *Style, 22*(1), 1–8.

Payne, T. E. (1997). *Describing Morphosyntax.* Cambridge University Press: Cambridge.

Prince, G. (1992). *Narratives as Theme: Studies in French Fiction.* London: University of Nebraska Press.

Roese, N. J., & Olson, J. M. (Eds.). (1995). *What Might Have Been: The Social Psychology of Counterfactual Thinking.* Mahwah, NJ: Lawrence Erlbaum Associates.

Roese, N. J., & Olson, J. M. (1996). Counterfactuals, Causal Attributions, and the Hindsight Bias: A Conceptual Integration. *Journal of Experimental Social Psychology, 32*(3), 197–227.

Scruggs, C. (1985). The Two Endings of "The French Lieutenant's Woman". *Modern Fiction Studies, 31*(1), 95–113.

Semino, E. (2002). A Cognitive Stylistic Approach to Mind Style in Narrative Fiction. In E. Semino & J. Culpeper (Eds.), *Cognitive Stylistics, Language and Cognition in Text Analysis.* Amsterdam: John Benjamins.

Semino, E. (2014). Pragmatic Failure, Mind Style and Characterisation in Fiction About Autism. *Language and Literature, 23*(2), 141–158.

Sliding Doors. (1998). Directed by Peter Howitt.

Stanzel, F. K. (1986). *A Theory of Narrative.* Cambridge: Cambridge University Press.

Stockwell, P. (2009). The Cognitive Poetics of Literary Resonance. *Language and Cognition, 1*(1), 25–44.

The Family Man. (2000). Directed by Brett Ratner.

The French Lieutenant's Woman. (1981). Directed by Karel Reisz.

Toolan, M. (2009). *Narrative Progression in the Short Story: A Corpus Stylistic Approach.* Amsterdam, The Netherlands: John Benjamins.

Warhol, R. R. (2005). Neonarrative; Or, How to Render the Unnarratable in Realist Fiction and Contemporary Film. In J. Phelan & P. Rabinowitz (Eds.), *A Companion to Narrative Theory* (pp. 220–231). Oxford: Blackwell.

Warhol, R. (2010). "What Might Have Been Is Not What Is": Dickens's Narrative Refusals. *Dickens Studies Annual, 41,* 45–60.

Warhol, R. (2013). It Is of Little Use for Me to Tell You: George Eliot's Narrative Refusals. In A. Anderson & H. E. Shaw (Eds.), *Companion to George Eliot* (pp. 46–61). London: Wiley.

Werth, P. (1999). *Text Worlds: Representing Conceptual Space in Discourse.* London: Longman.

Wolff, T. (1995, September 25). Bullet in the Brain. *The New Yorker*, pp. 82–83.

Wolff, T. (1996). Bullet in the Brain. In *The Night in Question* (pp. 200–206). London: Bloomsbury.

CHAPTER 6

Conclusion

Abstract This chapter concludes *Disnarration and the Unmentioned in Fact and Fiction* with a summary of some of the key discussion points in the book. The book's focus was to examine the unnarratable across a range of factual and fictional texts and understand why disnarrated modes of storytelling are so pervasive in all genres of storytelling. Analysis of experiential, personal stories, news and fictional narratives suggests there is a discourse of disnarration, while counterfactual divergence triggered by forking paths generate *what might have been* scenarios that are subsequently negated and disnarrated as only one path can be followed. Forking paths are a consequence of a network of plot options created by characters in the storyword making their own choices through metafictive devices beyond the role and responsibility of the narrator and author. *Disnarration and the Unmentioned in Fact and Fiction* confirms our continuing 'fascination of what doesn't happen' (Dannenberg in 2014) in a discussion that explores the roads not taken in these unconventional and tellable dimensions of stories.

Keywords Negation · Disnarration · News values · Forking paths · Counterfactual

M. Lambrou, *Disnarration and the Unmentioned in Fact and Fiction*,
https://doi.org/10.1057/978-1-137-50778-5_6

This book set out to examine the dimension of storytelling describing Prince's (1982) concept of the nonnarrated, unnarrated and disnarrated and why narratives developed with unconventional modes of storytelling where something ***does not happen*** are relevant, have narrativity and are tellable. Elements of a story can be left out for various reasons because it 'cannot be narrated or is not worth mentioning-either because it transgresses a law, or because it defies the powers of a particular narrator, or because it falls below the so-called threshold of narratability' (Prince 1992: 28). Warhol (2010: 46) extends Prince's dimensions with a discussion of 'narrative refusals' that convey 'what might have been and yet is not'. Her categories of ***subnarratable***, ***supranarratable***, ***antinarratable*** and ***paranarratable*** explain reasons for gaps and the unmentioned. Creative uses of negation in relation to what is narratable to express something that is marked as explicitly not there is one of the features that generates this mode of storytelling as does counterfactual thinking. Disnarration functions by foregrounding ways of creating the world by showing how plots and actions can follow alternative paths or be referred to and then rejected. The unnarrated and disnarrated allow narrative plots to develop along different, conceptual pathways to highlight how alternative, counterfactual experiences and actions can foreground hypothetical scenarios. Prince (1992: 34–35) claims that disnarration is not essential to narrative yet 'the insistence with which the disnarrated appears in countless "natural" narratives [...] as well as in historical and fictional discourse points to its narrative pertinence and significance', as the discussion in this book across a range of factual and fictional texts testify.

Chapter 2 presents various definitions of narrative that describe structure and function and the qualities that characterise this genre of text as being a narrative. A discussion of literary and linguistic models of narrative (Todorov, Forster, Labov, and Waletzky) contextualises the prototypical characteristics, where for example, a basic description is 'a perceived sequence of non-randomly connected events' (Toolan 2001: 8). It is from these events that we can learn something. Narratives are thought to be about problem-solving, conflict, interpersonal relations, human experience and about the temporality of experience (Ryan 2007). The element of Trouble with a capital 'T' (Bruner 1997) also appears to be a necessary factor for generating stories where other alternatives can be imagined. Narratives are expected to be temporal and connected by causality (whether perceived or inferred) while other, more abstract conditions include narrativity and tellability (or reportability in non-fictional narratives such as media narratives) where the relationship between audience expectation, perception and interpretation affect how readily a narrative is successfully perceived. A summary of Possible World Theory and the sub-worlds in Text World Theory to contextualise the alternative and hypothetical worlds that develop—whether as parallel universes or through counterfactual thinking—helps to visualise the concept of disnarration. As Bremond (1973) explains, every narrative function opens an alternative plot option so some paths are taken and not others, the others being disnarrated or choices not made, roads not taken, possibilities not actualized, goals not reached.

In Chapter 3, the focus on children's personal narratives based on *danger of death* and *fight* experiences, prompted numerous disnarrated scenarios where danger was described but avoided. Disnarrated experiences were expressed using degree adverbs, negation and the conditional *if+would* clause structures to express *what might have been* had the actions followed through, which Labov and Waletzky (1967) describe as comparators. The chapter began by asking why are experiences that do not happen and undermine the important quality of reportability which 'justifies the automatic reassignment of speaker role to the narrator' (Labov 1997: 406) narrated. The argument is that all experiences structured as narratives allow individuals to make sense of the world. Disnarrated experiences are negative experiences, and for children especially they are cognitively enabling as sharing experiences of potential danger is a necessary part of their socialisation. Individuals are able to reflect on and understand dangerous consequences and this point explains the prevalence of *near miss* stories published as headline news in news stories explored in Chapter 4. News stories also allow readers to make sense of the world they live in but news stories are also expected to adhere to a number of news values (Bell 1991) to be deemed newsworthy and justify publication. Stories about disnarrated events, popularly expressed as *near miss* stories, for example, describe events that could have happened but were avoided whether on a mass scale or with reference to an individual. Stylistically, disnarration in media news is communicated through textual gaps as ellipsis, negation, degree adverbs and conditional clauses. These dimensions of news stories are relevant because audiences are able to imagine and identify with the counterfactual consequences through news values such as *NEGATIVITY*, *PERSONALISATION* and *RECENCY* to visualise alternative outcomes. I also argue that the newsworthiness of these types of events is constructed in the imagination of the reader as much as through the linguistic choices in the text and that *THE DISNARRATED* to describe what 'could have happened' be added to the existing lists of news values.

In Chapter 5, the focus of the discussion turns to fictional texts and the analysis of disnarration in complex plot structures as marked dimensions of storytelling that offer glimpses of *what might have been*. The novel *The French Lieutenant's Woman* and the film *La La Land* rely on the use of creative metafictive devices for their endings, from forking paths (Borges 2000 [1944]) and the rejection of alternative possibilities. The plot twists generate counterfactual divergence as a consequence of narratives having a network of plot options (Bremond and Cancalon 1980). The central characters in both fictions—Charles and Sarah in *The French Lieutenant's Woman* and Mia and Sebastian in *La La Land*—have volition; they are able to consider their situation and make choices to follow their own hopes, wishes and desires, despite being constructs in the fictional world. Characters, therefore, can create their own plots and fates. Hypothetical scenarios are imagined and then disnarrated the moment they are rejected because characters can only progress along one plot option (unless you are Helen in the film *Sliding Doors* where two timelines are shown for most of the film). Disnarration in *Bullet in the Brain* is narrated through the marked use of negation to tell readers what Anders did not remember in his dying moments. Yet, by telling readers what Anders has forgotten, readers are simultaneously told details of significant moments in Anders's life through a process of 'negative uninformativeness' (Leech 1983: 101) as readers are invited to conceptualise the very thing that is negated. Readers retain the positive scenario rather than discard it and this proposition helps to construct a fuller understanding of what did not happen and what might have happened. The use of negation or negative polarity (Halliday and Matthiessen 2004) functions as a marked feature that draws attention to itself through patterns of (unexpected) regularity because positive polarity tends to be the norm. Disnarration is not only in the relationship between the text and plot structure, it is also present between the text and the reader: for Anders, his inability to recall important past events and to remember instead a trivial moment from his distant past is a defiant act of true characterization.

The paths not taken and those that are, create narrative interest, narrativity and tellability and gives characters and their storyworld dimensionality. Disnarration in all its forms allows plots and characters to speculate and follow paths and options that might happen in the real, discourse world of the audience where choices and possibilities are encountered on a daily basis. The pervasiveness of the disnarrated reflects their importance as a dimension of storytelling because 'Counterfactual scenarios are evocative not only because they illustrate attitudes, but because they often depict near, misses, lost opportunities, and foreclosed possibilities' (Riddle Harding 2007: 264). For all of these reasons, disnarration is central to storytelling, as I hope to have shown in this book.

References

Bell, A. (1991). *The Language of News Media*. Oxford: Blackwell.

Borges, J. L. (2000 [1944]). The Garden of Forking Paths. In *Collected Fictions* (A. Hurley, Trans., pp. 119–128). London: Penguin.

Bremond, C. (1973). *Logique du récit*. Paris: Editions du Seuil.

Bremond, C., & Cancalon, E. D. (1980). The Logic of Narrative Possibilities. *New Literary History, 11*(3), 387–411.

Bruner, J. (1997). Labov and Waletzky Thirty Years On. *Journal of Narrative and Life History, 7*(1–4), 61–68.

Dannenberg, H. P. (2014). Gerald Prince and the Fascination of What Doesn't Happen. *Narrative, 22*(3), 304–311.

Halliday, M. A. K., & Matthiessen, C. M. I. M. (2004). *An Introduction to Functional Grammar* (3rd ed.). London: Edward Arnold.

Labov, W. (1997). Further Steps in Narrative Analysis. *Journal of Narrative and Life History, 7*(1–4), 395–415.

Labov, W., & Waletzky, J. (1967). Narrative Analysis: Oral Versions of Personal Experience. In J. Holm (Ed.), *Essays on the Verbal and Visual Arts* (pp. 12–44). Seattle: University of Washington Press.

Leech, G. (1983). *The Principles of Pragmatics*. Harlow: Longman.

Prince, G. (1982). *Narratology: The Form and Functioning of Narrative*. Berlin: Mouton.

Prince, G. (1992). *Narratives as Theme: Studies in French Fiction*. London: University of Nebraska Press.

Riddle Harding, J. (2007). Evaluative Stance and Counterfactuals in Language and Literature. *Language and Literature, 16*(3), 263–280.

Ryan, M. (2007). Toward a Definition of Narrative. In D. Herman (Ed.), *The Cambridge Companion to Narrative* (Cambridge Companions to Literature, pp. 22–36). Cambridge: Cambridge University Press.

Toolan, M. J. (2001). *Narrative: A Critical Linguistic Introduction* (2nd ed.). London: Routledge.

Warhol, R. (2010). "What Might Have Been Is Not What Is": Dickens's Narrative Refusals. *Dickens Studies Annual, 41*, 45–60.

Appendix: Transcription Conventions

?	question or uncertainty
!	Surprise
WORDS IN CAPITALS	emphatic stress and/or increase in volume
" "	indicates direct speech
"*italics*"	captures the marked change in voice quality in direct speech
[ ]	indecipherable speech
[laughs]	paralinguistic and non-verbal information
=	interruption
…	pauses of under 3 seconds
-dash	false start/restart
a-and	elongation of word

M. Lambrou, *Disnarration and the Unmentioned in Fact and Fiction*,
https://doi.org/10.1057/978-1-137-50778-5

References

Abbott, H. P. (2005). Closure. In D. Herman, M. Jahn, & M.-L. Ryan (Eds.), *Routledge Encyclopedia of Narrative Theory* (pp. 65–66). London: Routledge.

Abbott, H. P. (2008). *The Cambridge Introduction to Narrative* (2nd ed.). Cambridge: Cambridge University Press.

Abbott, H. P. (2013). *Real Mysteries, Narrative and the Unknowable.* Columbus, OH: Ohio State University.

Alber, J. (2013). Unnatural Narrative. In P. Hühn, J. C. Meister, J. Pier, & W. Schmid (Eds.), *The Living Handbook of Narratology.* Hamburg: Hamburg University. Available at http://www.lhn.uni-hamburg.de/article/unnatural-narrative. Accessed 24 October 2018.

Alber, J., Iversen, S., Nielsen, H. S., & Richardson, B. (2010). Unnatural Narratives, Unnatural Narratology: Beyond Mimetic Models. *Narrative 18*(2), 113–136.

Austen, J. (1817). *Northanger Abbey.* London: John Murray.

Austen, J. (2003). *Northanger Abbey.* London: Penguin.

Barnes, J. (2011). *The Sense of an Ending.* New York: Alfred A. Knopf.

Barnett, L. (2015). *The Versions of Us.* London: Weidenfeld & Nicolson.

Baroni, R. (2016). Virtualities of Plot and Dynamics of Re-reading. In R. Baroni & F. Revaz (Eds.), *Narrative Sequence in Contemporary Narratologies* (pp. 87–106). Columbus: Ohio State University Press.

Baroni, R. (2017). The Garden of Forking Paths: Virtualities and Challenges for Contemporary Narratology. In P. K. Hansen, J. Pier, P. Roussin, & W. Schmid (dir.), *Emerging Vectors of Narratology* (pp. 247–263). Berlin: de Gruyter, coll. Narratologia.

Bednarek, M. (2006) *Evaluation in Media Discourse: Analysis of a Newspaper Corpus.* London: Continuum.

M. Lambrou, *Disnarration and the Unmentioned in Fact and Fiction*,
https://doi.org/10.1057/978-1-137-50778-5

Bednarek, M., & Caple, H. (2014). Why Do News Values Matter? Towards a New Methodological Framework for Analysing News Discourse in Critical Discourse Analysis and Beyond. *Discourse and Society, 25*(2), 135–158.

Bell, A. (1991). *The Language of News Media*. Oxford: Blackwell.

Bell, A. (1998). The Discourse Structure of News Stories. In A. Bell & P. Garrett (Eds.), *Approaches to Media Discourse* (pp. 64–104). Oxford: Blackwell.

Bell, A. (2010). *The Possible Worlds of Hypertext Fiction*. Basingstoke: Palgrave-Macmillan.

Bell, A. (2016). 'I Felt Like I'd Stepped Out of a Different Reality': Possible Worlds Theory, Metalepsis and Digital Fiction. In J. Gavins & E. Lahey (Eds.), *World Building: Discourse in the Mind* (pp. 15–32). London: Bloomsbury.

Birke, D., Butter, M., & Köppe, T. (2001). Introduction: England Win. In D. Birke, M. Butter, & T. Köppe (Eds.), *Counterfactual Thinking/Counterfactual Writing* (p. 2). Berlin: Walter de Gruyter.

Borges, J. L. (2000 [1944]). The Garden of Forking Paths. In *Collected Fictions* (A. Hurley, Trans., pp. 119–128). London: Penguin.

Branigan, E. (1992). *Narrative Comprehension and Film*. London and New York: Routledge.

Bremond, C. (1973). *Logique du récit*. Paris: Editions du Seuil.

Bremond, C., & Cancalon, E. D. (1980). The Logic of Narrative Possibilities. *New Literary History, 11*(3), 387–411.

Bruner, J. (1986). *Actual Minds, Possible Worlds*. Cambridge, MA: Harvard University Press.

Bruner, J. (1991). The Narrative Construction of 'Reality'. *Critical Inquiry, 18*, 1–21.

Bruner, J. (1997). Labov and Waletzky Thirty Years On. *Journal of Narrative and Life History, 7*(1–4), 61–68.

Burke, K. (1945). *A Grammar of Motives*. New York: Prentice Hall.

Chatman, S. (1978). *Story and Discourse: Narrative Structure in Fiction and Film*. Ithaca, NY: Cornell University Press.

Chatman, S. (1990). *Coming to Terms: The Rhetoric of Narrative in Fiction and Film*. Ithaca: Cornell University Press.

Chopin, K. (1993 [1899]). *The Awakening* (N. A. Walker, Ed.). Boston: Bedford Books.

Cobley, P. (2014). *Narrative* (2nd ed.). London: Routledge.

Culler, J. (1997). *Literary Theory*. Oxford: Oxford University Press.

Culpeper, J. (2001). *Language and Characterisation: People in Plays and Other Texts*. London: Routledge.

Dancygier, B. (2012). *The Language of Stories: A Cognitive Approach*. Cambridge: Cambridge University Press.

Dannenberg, H. P. (2008). *Coincidence and Counterfactuality: Plotting Time and Space in Narrative Fiction*. Lincoln and London: University of Nebraska Press.

Dannenberg, H. P. (2014). Gerald Prince and the Fascination of What Doesn't Happen. *Narrative, 22*(3), 304–311.

Davis, W. A., Jr. (1997). The Rape of Tess: Hardy, English Law, and the Case for Sexual Assault. *Nineteenth-Century Literature, 52*(2), 221–231.

Dawson, P. (2018, April 18–22). *Creativity-Narrativity-Fictionality: A Critical Genealogy*. Paper presented to the International Conference on Narrative, McGill University, Montreal.

Debnath, N. (2016). *I Could Have Killed Them All Sky News Reporter Slated over Bizarre Terrorism Report*. Express.co.uk. Available at https://www.express.co.uk/showbiz/tv-radio/694427/Sky-News-Martin-Brunt-Twitter-Normandy. Accessed 31 October 2018.

Dick, P. K. (2015 [1962]). *The Man in the High Castle*. London: Penguin.

Dickens, C. (1843). *A Christmas Carol*. London: Chapman & Hall.

Doležel, L. (1998). *Heterocosmica: Fiction and Possible Worlds*. Baltimore: Johns Hopkins University Press.

Duszak, A. (1991). Schematic and Topical Categories in News Story Reconstruction. *Text, 11*, 503–522.

Evans, H. (1972). *Editing and Design. A Five-Volume Manual of English, Typography and Layout. Book One. Newsman's English*. London: Heinemann.

Fludernik, M. (1996). *Towards a 'Natural' Narratology*. London: Routledge.

Fludernik, M. (2009). *An Introduction to Narratology*. London: Routledge.

Forster, E. M. (1927). *Aspects of the Novel*. London: Edward Arnold.

Fowler, R. (1977). *Linguistics and The Novel*. London: Methuen.

Fowles, J. (1969). *The French Lieutenant's Woman*. London: Vintage.

Galtung, J., & Ruge, M. H. (1965). The Structure of Foreign News: The Presentation of the Congo, Cuba and Cyprus in Four Norwegian newspapers. *Journal of Peace Research, 2*(1), 64–90.

Gavins, J. (2007). *Text World Theory: An Introduction*. Edinburgh: Edinburgh University Press.

Gavins, J., & Lahey, E. (2016). *World Building: Discourse in the Mind*. London: Bloomsbury.

Genette, G. (1980 [1972]). *Narrative Discourse: An Essay on Method*. Ithaca, NY: Cornell University Press.

Genette, G. (1988 [1983]). *Narrative Discourse Revisited*. Ithaca, NY: Cornell University Press.

Giovanelli, M. (2013). *Text World Theory and Keats' Poetry: The Cognitive Poetics of Desire, Dreams and Nightmares*. London: Bloomsbury.

Green, H. (1929). *Living*. London: Harvill Harper Collins.

Gregoriou, C. (2007). *Deviance in Contemporary Crime Fiction*. Basingstoke: Palgrave Macmillan.

Grice, H. P. (1975). Logic and Conversation. In P. Cole & J. Morgan (Eds.), *Syntax and Semantics* (Vol. 3, pp. 41–58). New York: Academic Press.

Halliday, M. A. K., & Matthiessen, C. M. I. M. (2004). *An Introduction to Functional Grammar* (3rd ed.). London: Edward Arnold.

Hansen, K. R. (2016). News from the Future: A Corpus Linguistic Analysis of Future-Orientated, Unreal and Counterfactual News Discourse. *Discourse & Communication, 10*(2), 115–136.

Hanson, C. (1989). "Things Out of Words": Towards a Poetics of Short Fiction. In C. Hanson (Ed.), *Rereading the Short Story* (pp. 22–23). Basingstoke: Macmillan.

Harcup, T. (2009). *Journalism, Principles and Practice* (2nd ed.). London: Sage.

Harcup, T., & O'Neill, D. (2001). What Is News? Galtung and Ruge Revisited. *Journalism Studies, 2*(2), 261–280.

Hardy, T. (1891). *Tess of the d'Urbervilles*. London: James R. Osgood. McIlvaine & Co.

Hardy, D. (2003). *Narrating Knowledge in Flannery O'Connor's Fiction*. Columbia: University of South Carolina Press.

Hardy, D. (2005). Towards a Stylistic Typology of Narrative Gaps: Knowledge Gapping in Flannery O'Connor's Fiction. *Language and Literature, 14*(4), 363–375.

Herman, D. (2002). *Story Logic*. London: University of Nebraska Press.

Herman, D. (2003). Stories as a Tool for Thinking. In D. Herman (Ed.), *Narrative Theory and the Cognitive Sciences* (pp. 163–192). Stanford: CSLI Publications.

Herman, D. (Ed.). (2007). *The Cambridge Companion to Narrative*. Cambridge: Cambridge University Press.

Iser, W. (1974). *The Implied Reader: Patterns of Communication in Prose Fiction from Bunyan to Beckett*. Baltimore: John Hopkins University Press.

Iser, W. (1978). *The Act of Reading*. London: Routledge.

It's a Wonderful Life. (1946). Directed by Frank Capra.

Jeffries, L. (2010). *Critical Stylistics*. London: Palgrave Macmillan.

Jeffries, L., & McIntyre, D. (2010). *Stylistics*. Cambridge: Cambridge University Press.

Joyce, J. (1914). *Dubliners*. London: Grant Richards Ltd.

Karttunen, L. (2008). A Sociostylistic Perspective on Negatives and the Disnarrated: Lahiri, Roy, Rushdie. *Partial Answers: Journal of Literature and the History of Ideas, 6*(2), 419–441.

Kelly, R. M. (2003). Introduction. In C. Dickens (Ed.), *A Christmas Carol* (pp. 9–30). Ontario: Broadway Press.

Kermode, F. (1968). *The Sense of an Ending*. Oxford: Oxford University Press.

Labov, W. (1972). *Language in the Inner City*. Philadelphia: University of Pennsylvania Press.

Labov, W. (1997). Further Steps in Narrative Analysis. *Journal of Narrative and Life History, 7*(1–4), 395–415.

Labov, W., & Waletzky, J. (1967). Narrative Analysis: Oral Versions of Personal Experience. In J. Holm (Ed.), *Essays on the Verbal and Visual Arts* (pp. 12–44). Seattle: University of Washington Press.

La La Land. (2016). Directed by Damien Chazelle.

Lakoff, G., & Johnson, M. (1980). *Metaphors We Live By*. Chicago: University of Chicago Press.

Lambrou, M. (2003). Collaborative Oral Narratives of General Experience: When an Interview Becomes a Conversation. *Language and Literature, 12*(2), 153–174.

Lambrou, M. (2005). *Story Patterns in Oral Narratives: A Variationist Critique of Labov and Waletzky's Model of Narrative Schemas* (Unpublished PhD thesis). Middlesex University, London.

Lambrou, M. (2007). Oral Accounts of Personal Experiences: When Is a Narrative a Recount?' In M. Lambrou & P. Stockwell (Eds.), *Contemporary Stylistics* (pp. 195–208). London: Continuum.

Lambrou, M. (2018). "*La La Land*": Counterfactuality, Disnarration and the forked (motorway) path. In R. Page, B. Busse, & N. Nørgaard (Eds.), *Rethinking Language, Text and Context: Interdisciplinary Research in Stylistics in Honour of Michael Toolan* (pp. 29–42). London: Routledge.

Lambrou, M. (2019). Metalepsis, Counterfactuality and Being Led Up the "Forked" Garden Path: 'Manipulating' Readers in Fiction. In S. Sorline (Ed.), *Stylistic Manipulation of the Reader in Contemporary Literature*. London: Bloomsbury.

Lawler, J. (2010). Negation and Negative Polarity. In P. C. Hogan (Ed.), *Cambridge Encyclopedia of the Language Sciences* (pp. 554–555). Cambridge: Cambridge University Press.

Leech, G. (1983). *The Principles of Pragmatics*. Harlow: Longman.

Leibniz, G. W. (1952 [1710]). *Theodicy* (E. M. Huggard, Trans.). London: Routledge.

Lewis, D. (1978). Truth in Fiction. *American Philosophical Quarterly, 1*, 37–46.

Lewis, D. (1986). *On the Plurality of Worlds*. Oxford: Blackwell.

Lindholm, H. (2003). Perhaps She Had Not Told Him All the Story: The Disnarrated in James Joyce's Dubliners. In F. Iftekharuddin, J. Boyden, M. Rohrberger, & J. Claudet (Eds.), *The Postmodern Short Story: Forms and Issues* (pp. 207–219). Westport, CT: Praeger.

Lule, J. (2001). *Daily News, Eternal Stories: The Mythological Role of Journalism*. New York: Guilford Press.

Lutz, B., & Wodak, R. (1987). *Information für Informierte: Linguistische Studien zu Verständlichkeit und Verstehen von Hörfunknachrichten*. Vienna: Verlag der Österreichischen Akademie der Wissenschaften.

Mandler, J., Scribner, S., Cole, M., & DeForrest, M. (1980). Cross-Cultural Invariance in Story Recall. *Child Development, 51*, 19–26.

Margolin, U. (1990). The What, the When, and the How of Being a Character in Literary Narrative. *Style, 24*(3), 453–468.

Markman, K. D., & McMullen, M. N. (2014). Reflective and Evaluative Modes of Mental Simulation. In D. R. Mandel, D. J. Hilton, & P. Catellani (Eds.), *The Psychology of Counterfactual Thinking* (pp. 77–93). London: Routledge.

McEwan, I. (2001). *Atonement*. London: Jonathan Cape.

Meng, K. (1992). Narrating and Listening in kindergarten. *Journal of Narrative and Life History, 2*(3), 235–276.

Meyer, S. (2006). *Twilight*. London: Atom.

Michotte, M. (1963 [1946]). *The Perception of Causality* (T. R. Miles & E. Miles, Trans.). London: Methuen.

Miller, P. (1995). Personal Storytelling in Everyday Life: Social and Cultural Perspectives. In *Knowledge and Memory: The Real Story: Advances in Social Cognition* (Vol. 8, pp. 177–184). London, UK: Lawrence Erlbaum Associates.

Miller, P., & Moore, B. B. (1989). Narrative Conjunctions of Caregiver and Child: A Comparative Perspective on Socialization Through Stories. *Ethos: Journal of the Society for Psychological Anthropology, 17*(4), 428–449.

Miller, P. J., Fung, J., & Mintz, J. (1996). Self-Construction Through Narrative Practices: A Chinese and American Comparison of Early Socialization. *Ethos, 24*(2), 237–280.

Montoro, R. (2018). The Creative Use of Absences, A Corpus Stylistic Approach to Henry Green's *Living*. *International Journal of Corpus Linguistics, 23*(3), 279–310.

Mosher, H. F., Jr. (1993). The Narrated and Its Negatives: The Nonnarrated and the Disnarrated in Joyce's *Dubliners*. *Style, 27*, 407–427.

Mukařovsky, J. (1964 [1932]). Standard Language and Poetic Language. In P. Garvin (Ed.), *A Prague School Reader on Aesthetics, Literary Structure and Style* (pp. 17–30). Washington, DC: Georgetown University Press.

Nahajec, L. (2014). Negation, Expectation and Characterisation: Analysing the Role of Negation in Character Construction in *to Kill a Mockingbird* (Lee 1960) and *Stark* (Elton 1989). In S. Chapman & B. Clark (Eds.), *Pragmatic Literary Stylistics* (pp. 111–131). London: Palgrave Macmillan.

Niblock, S. (2005). Practice and Theory: What Is News? In R. Keeble (Ed.), *Print Journalism, A Critical Introduction*. London: Routledge.

Nodelman, P. (1992). *The Pleasure of Children's Literature*. London: Longman.

Nørgaard, N. (2007). Disordered Collarettes and Uncovered Tables: Negative Polarity as a Stylistic Device' in Joyce's 'Two Gallants'. *Journal of Literary Semantics, 36*(1), 35–52.

Ochs, E., & Capps, L. (2001). *Living Narrative*. Cambridge, MA: Harvard University Press.

Pape, W. (1992). Happy Endings in a World of Misery: A Literary Convention Between Social Constraints and Utopia in Children's and Adult Literature. *Poetics Today, 13*(1), 179–196.

Payne, T. E. (1997). *Describing Morphosyntax*. Cambridge: Cambridge University Press.

Phelan, J. (2017). *Somebody Telling Somebody Else, a Rhetorical Poetics of Narrative*. Columbus: Ohio State Press.

Popova, Y. (2015a). Narrativity. In V. Sotirova (Ed.), *The Bloomsbury Companion to Stylistic* (pp. 488–506). London: Routledge.

Popova, Y. (2015b). *Stories, Meaning and Experience: Narrativity and Enaction*. London: Routledge.

Pratt, M. L. (1994) The Short Story: The Long and the Short of It. In C. E. May (Ed.), *The New Short Story Theories* (pp. 91–113). Columbus: Ohio University Press.

Prince, G. (1982). *Narratology: The Form and Functioning of Narrative*. Berlin: Mouton.

Prince, G. (1988). The 'Disnarrated'. *Style, 22*(1), 1–8.

Prince, G. (1992). *Narratives as Theme: Studies in French Fiction*. London: University of Nebraska Press.

Prince, G. (2003). *Dictionary of Narratology*. Lincoln and London: University of Nebraska Press.

Prince, G. (2005). Narrativity. In D. Herman, M. Jahn, & M.-L. Ryan (Eds.), *Routledge Encyclopedia of Narrative Theory* (pp. 387–388). London: Routledge.

Propp, V. (1968 [1928]). *Morphology of the Folktale*. Austin: University of Texas Press.

Rabinowitz, P. (1987). *Before Reading: Narrative Conventions and the Politics of Interpretation*. Columbus: Ohio State Press.

Ricouer, P. (1980). Narrative Time. In W. J. T Mitchell (Ed.), *On Narrative* (pp. 165–186). Chicago: Chicago University Press.

Riddle Harding, J. (2007). Evaluative Stance and Counterfactuals in Language and Literature. *Language and Literature, 16*(3), 263–280.

Robinson, A. (2011). *Narrating the Past: Histography, Memory and the Contemporary Novel*. Basingstoke: Palgrave, Macmillan.

Roese, N. J., & Olson, J. M. (Eds.). (1995a). *What Might Have Been: The Social Psychology of Counterfactual Thinking*. Mahwah, NJ: Lawrence Erlbaum Associates.

Roese, N. J., & Olson, J. M. (Eds.). (1995b). Counterfactual Thinking: A Critical Overview. In *What Might Have Been: The Social Psychology of Counterfactual Thinking*. Hillsdale, NJ: Lawrence Erlbaum Associates.

Roese, N. J., & Olson, J. M. (1996). Counterfactuals, Causal Attributions, and the Hindsight Bias: A Conceptual Integration. *Journal of Experimental Social Psychology, 32*(3), 197–227.

Rosaler, R. (2016). *Conspicuous Silences.* Oxford: Oxford University Press.

Ryan, M.-L. (1991). *Possible Worlds, Artificial Intelligence, and Narrative Theory*. Bloomington: Indiana University Press.

Ryan, M.-L. (2005). Tellability. In D. Herman, M. Jahn, & M.-L. Ryan (Eds.), *Routledge Encyclopedia of Narrative Theory* (pp. 589–91). London: Routledge.

Ryan, M. (2007). Toward a Definition of Narrative. In D. Herman (Ed.), *The Cambridge Companion to Narrative* (Cambridge Companions to Literature, pp. 22–36). Cambridge: Cambridge University Press.

Ryan, M.-L. (2013). Possible Worlds. In P. Hühn, J. C. Meister, J. Pier, & W. Schmid (Eds.), *The Living Handbook of Narratology.* Hamburg: Hamburg University. http://www.lhn.uni-hamburg.de/article/possible-worlds. Accessed 8 October 2017.

Ryan, M.-L. (2014). Possible Worlds. In P. Hühn, J. C. Meister, J. Pier, & W. Schmid (Eds.), *Handbook of Narratology* (pp. 726–742). Berlin and Boston: De Gruyter.

Sacks, H. (1992). *Lectures on Conversation.* Oxford: Blackwell.

Sacks, H., Schegloff, E. A., & Jefferson, G. (1974). A Simplest Systematics for the Organization of Turn-Taking for Conversation. *Language, 50*(4), 696–735.

Schank, R. C., & Abelson, R. P. (1995). Knowledge and Memory: The Real Story. In R. S. Wyer Jr. (Ed.), *Knowledge and Memory: The Real Story* (pp. 220–231). Hillsdale, NJ: Lawrence Erlbaum Associates.

Scholes, R., & Kellogg, R. (1966). *The Nature of Narrative.* New York: Oxford University Press.

Scruggs, C. (1985). The Two Endings of "The French Lieutenant's Woman". *Modern Fiction Studies, 31*(1), 95–113.

Semino, E. (2002). A Cognitive Stylistic Approach to Mind Style in Narrative Fiction. In E. Semino & J. Culpeper (Eds.), *Cognitive Stylistics, Language and Cognition in Text Analysis.* Amsterdam: John Benjamins.

Semino, E. (2005). Possible Worlds: Stylistics Applications. In K. Brown (Ed.), *Elsevier Encyclopaedia of Language and Linguistics* (pp. 777–782). London: Elsevier.

Semino, E. (2014). Pragmatic Failure, Mind Style and Characterisation in Fiction About Autism. *Language and Literature, 23*(2), 141–158.

Shklovsky, V. (1991 [1925]). *Theory of Prose* (V. B. Sher, Trans.). Illinois State University, Dalkey Archive Press.

Simpson, P., & Canning, P. (2014). Action and event. In P. Stockwell & S. Whitely (Eds.), *The Cambridge Handbook of Stylistics* (pp. 281–299). Cambridge: Cambridge University Press.

Sliding Doors. (1998). Directed by Peter Howitt.

Spencer-Thomas, O. (2005). *News Values*. http://www.owenspencer-thomas.com/journalism/newsvalues. Accessed 12 November 2017.

Spolsky, E. (2005). Gapping. In D. Herman, M. Jahn, & M.-L. Ryan (Eds.), *Routledge Encyclopedia of Narrative Theory* (pp. 193–194). London: Routledge.

Sterne, L. (1996 [1759]). *The Life and Opinions of Tristram Shandy, Gentleman*. York: R. & J. Dodsley.

Stanzel, F. K. (1986). *A Theory of Narrative*. Cambridge: Cambridge University Press.

Sternberg, M. (2010). Narrativity: From Objectivist to Functional Paradigm. *Poetics Today, 31*, 507–659.

Stockwell, P. (2002). *Cognitive Poetics*. London: Routledge.

Stockwell, P. (2009). The Cognitive Poetics of Literary Resonance. *Language and Cognition, 1*(1), 25–44.

Thackeray, W. M. (1848). *Vanity Fair*. London: Bradbury and Evans.

The Family Man. (2000). Directed by Brett Ratner.

The French Lieutenant's Woman. (1981). Directed by Karel Reisz.

Thompson, G. (1996). *Introducing Functional Grammar*. London: Arnold.

Todorov, T. (1977).*The Poetics of Prose*. Oxford: Blackwell.

Toolan, M. J. (2001). *Narrative, A Critical Linguistic Introduction* (2nd ed.). London: Routledge.

Toolan, M. (2009). *Narrative Progression in the Short Story: A Corpus Stylistic Approach*. Amsterdam, The Netherlands: John Benjamins.

Twain, M. (1924) *Mark Twain*'s *Autobiography* (Vol. 1). New York and London: Harper & Brothers.

Walsh, T. (1998). *The Dark Matter of Words: Absence, Unknowing, and Emptiness in Literature*. Carbondale: University of Southern Illinois Press.

Warhol, R. R. (2005). Neonarrative; Or, How to Render the Unnarratable in Realist Fiction and Contemporary Film. In J. Phelan & P. Rabinowitz (Eds.), *A Companion to Narrative Theory* (pp. 220–231). Oxford: Blackwell.

Warhol, R. (2007). Narrative Refusals and Generic Transformation in Austen and James: What Doesn't Happen in Northanger Abbey and Spoils of Poynton. *Henry James Review, 28*(3), 259–268.

Warhol, R. (2010). "What Might Have Been Is Not What Is": Dickens's Narrative Refusals. *Dickens Studies Annual, 41*, 45–60.

Warhol, R. (2013). It Is of Little Use for Me to Tell You: George Eliot's Narrative Refusals. In A. Anderson & H. E. Shaw (Eds.), *Companion to George Eliot* (pp. 46–61). London: Wiley.

Waugh, P. (1984). *Metafiction: The Theory and Practice of Self-Conscious Fiction.* New York: Methuen.

Werth, P. (1999). *Text Worlds: Representing Conceptual Space in Discourse.* London: Longman.

Wilensky, R. (1983). Story Grammars Versus Story Points. *Behavioral and Brain Sciences, 6*, 579–623.

Wilson, P. (2000). *Mind the Gap, Ellipsis and Stylistic Variation in Spoken and Written English.* Harlow, Essex: Pearson Education Limited.

Wolff, T. (1995, September 25). Bullet in the Brain. *The New Yorker*, pp. 82–83.

Wolff, T. (1996). 'Bullet in the Brain'. In *The Night in Question* (pp. 200–206). Bloomsbury: London.

Websites

https://www.bbc.co.uk/news/world-middle-east-34524403. Accessed 7 May 2017.

https://www.bbc.co.uk/news/business-32622534. Accessed 8 May 2017.

http://www.dailymail.co.uk/news/article-2560452/Near-miss-A-motorised-paraglider-misses-EasyJet-passenger-plane-150ft.html. Accessed 1 July 2015.

https://www.dailymail.co.uk/news/article-2863948/Heathrow-Airbus-near-miss-drone-ghosted-Britain-s-biggest-airport-undetected-air-traffic-control.html. Accessed 10 October 2017.

https://www.express.co.uk/showbiz/tv-radio/694427/Sky-News-Martin-Brunt-Twitter-Normandy. Accessed 12 October 2017.

https://www.theguardian.com/world/2013/sep/20/usaf-atomic-bomb-north-carolina-1961. Accessed September 2018.

http://www.la-screenwriter.com/wp-content/uploads/2017/02/LA-LA-Land.pdf. Accessed 7 May 2017.

https://www.reddit.com/r/FanTheories/comments/5wavk7/la_la_land_time_travel_and_alternate_universes/. Accessed 7 May 2017.

Index

M. Lambrou, *Disnarration and the Unmentioned in Fact and Fiction*,
https://doi.org/10.1057/978-1-137-50778-5